PJ NORRIS AND THE HAMLET WITH THE MONSTER SITUATION

RELATED TITLES BY S. USHER EVANS

FIREWING INVESTIGATIONS
PJ Norris and the Town with the Butterfly Problem
PJ Norris and the Village with the Gnome Dilemma
PJ Norris and the Hamlet with the Monster Situation

THE WEARY DRAGON INN SERIES
Ale and Amnesia *(Newsletter Exclusive)*
Drinks and Sinkholes
Fiends and Festivals
Secrets and Snowflakes
Beasts and Baking
Magic and Molemen
Veils and Villains
Zealots and Zeniths
Campaigns and Curses
Perils and Potions
Royals and Ruses

THE POBYD PERFECTIONS SERIES
A Drizzle of Magic
A Splash of Arcana
A Dash of Sorcery

PJ NORRIS AND THE HAMLET

with the MONSTER SITUATION

FIREWING INVESTIGATIONS

BOOK THREE

S. USHER EVANS

Sun's Golden Ray Publishing

PENSACOLA, FL

Version Date: 9/8/25

ISBN: 978-1-965767-22-1
Retail Version

Cover Design and Chapter Typography by Sun's Golden Ray Publishing
Map Designed by Frederick Kroner with Stardust Book Services
Line Editing by Danielle Fine, By Definition Editing
Proofreading by Lisa Henson, Capitol Editing

Sun's Golden Ray Publishing
Pensacola, FL
www.sgr-pub.com

For ordering information, please visit
www.sgr-pub.com/orders

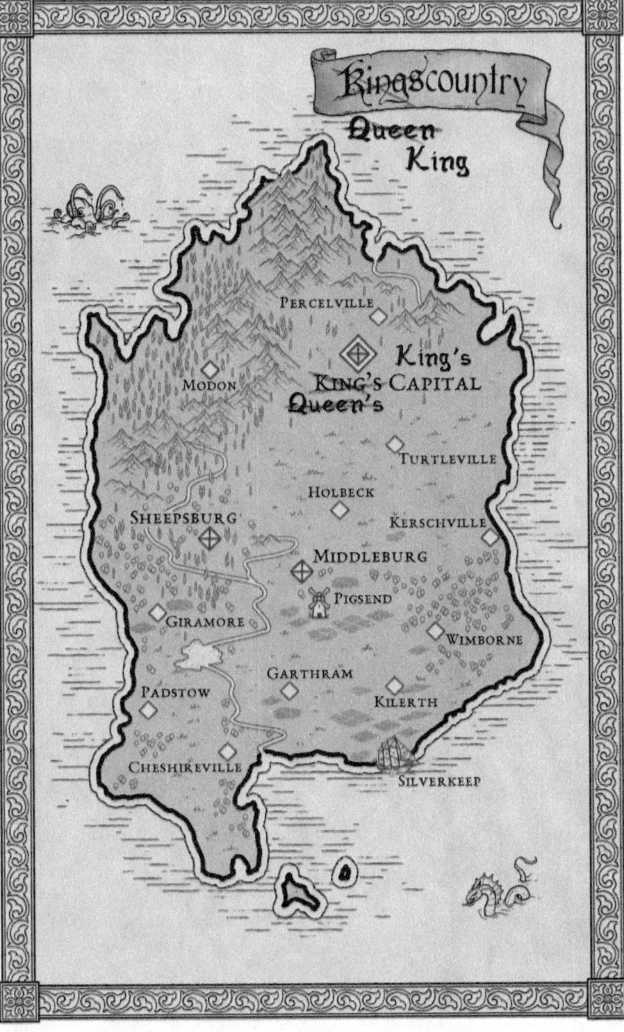

Kingscountry
Queen
King
PERCELVILLE
King's
KING'S CAPITAL
Queen's
MODON
TURTLEVILLE
HOLBECK
SHEEPSBURG
KERSCHVILLE
MIDDLEBURG
PIGSEND
GIRAMORE
WIMBORNE
GARTHRAM
PADSTOW
KILERTH
CHESHIREVILLE
SILVERKEEP

CHAPTER ONE

"I, erm, think that's just how they're supposed to look."

PJ Norris struggled to keep a straight face as the farmer showed him the interesting bulge between his goat's legs. While it certainly might've been *unique*, it didn't set off his magic senses whatsoever.

The farmer deflated. "Well, shoot. I was hoping to sell him for some extra coin. You think I could still pass him off as a magical goat?"

"I think you can do whatever you set your mind to." Grant Hamblin, PJ's best friend and travel partner, slapped the farmer on the shoulder. "People believe all sorts of nonsensical stuff. Especially now that magic's legal again."

PJ doubted that, and he also doubted the farmer would be able to pass his very normal goat off as anything more than a curiosity. But he'd halfway expected that when the farmer had waved him down as they were leaving his neighbor's house (where they'd been asked to inspect a pair of curiously feathered chickens).

Word had started to spread, at least among the farmers near the small mining village of Padstow, that a pair of magical investigators were traveling the country, solving magical problems. PJ and Grant had earned that notoriety by helping not one but two towns so far. First had been the town of Gilramore, which had been plagued by a spate of butterfly attacks. And then, most recently, Padstow, whose magical mine had been hit by a series of surges, which had almost caused the gnomes who bolstered the entire economy to leave.

In both cases, the causes of the incidents had been ancillary to the larger problems in town. PJ had helped a witch who'd been hiding for the better part of seven years reintegrate with her friends (and ensured a nasty bully had been made to feel most unwelcome), and he'd managed to find a solution for the gnomes, who would be forced to leave anyway when the magic fueling their mine ran out. That, more than finding the fairy who'd been attacking the town or the farmer trying to pad his pockets, had been the most rewarding part of his job.

That being said, they hadn't made it very far out of Padstow before other farmers who'd heard of their exploits came to the road, hoping to see them. First, there'd been a farmer who wondered if something magical was killing his crops (it wasn't). Then, another farmer who wanted PJ to search his land for magic, in case he could entice the gnomes to move to his land (there wasn't any to be found). Then the farmer with the curious chickens and now the current one, who'd been loitering outside his neighbor's house.

All along the way, Grant had been collecting silvers in exchange for their observations. As they left this latest farmer, Grant greedily counted the coins in his pouch, grinning like a madman now that he had his own coin to spend.

"You really didn't have to charge them," PJ said. "It's not like we're struggling for money."

"It's not about the money, Peej. It's about making sure they really want to bug us," Grant said. "I don't know about you, but I'm looking at the sun, and I'm looking at the surrounding area, and I'm not seeing a whole lotta towns. So if we're going to stop, we need to make potentially sleeping outside tonight worth our while."

The sun was still overhead, so they had time to

find a place. But it was useless to argue, so PJ kept his opinions to himself. The days were growing shorter as winter approached, so Grant wasn't wrong to want to filter out some unnecessary stops. Still, they didn't exactly have a destination in mind, so any town with an inn and a place to eat would suffice—and if there happened to be a dragon shifter in need of help there, all the better.

PJ, a shifter himself, had been given the task of searching the country by a trio of eccentric old women he called the grannies. They'd warned him the quest might take some time, as in their seven years of searching, he was the only one they'd found. But they'd also encouraged him to use his dragon powers for good, helping to right wrongs where he saw them and fixing problems as he was able. It had made the lack of dragon discovery a bit easier to swallow, though he sometimes wondered if he was wasting his time with gnomes and butterflies when there were larger problems to tackle.

As the hours wore on, and the sun sank on a still-vacant landscape, PJ couldn't help but worry Grant might've been right to try to speed things along. But just as he was ready to suggest they should find a soft spot on the ground, they came across a half-fallen sign with an arrow pointing off the main road toward a less-used one heading north. The paint had all but chipped off the wood, but it was still legible.

Cheshireville Inn This Way

Softest (and only) beds from here to Caldona

"Where's Caldona?" PJ asked.

"I think it's on the tip of the southern peninsula," Grant said, scratching his head. "I was always terrible with geography."

"Cheshireville," PJ murmured to himself. "I think the ogres stayed there while they were hiding from the queen. Said it was a magical forest of some kind."

"Magical forests probably have magical problems," Grant said with a slow nod.

"And there's an inn," PJ said. "Probably dinner, too. Should we check it out?"

Grant studied the sign with a frown. "I dunno. This thing doesn't look like it's been touched in a few years. Can you have Tim take a look ahead and make sure we're not walking into an abandoned town?"

"If you like," PJ said, though based on the hour, beggars couldn't be too choosy. "Erm, Tim? Do you see anything worth checking out over there?"

The dragon who lived in PJ's mind—affectionately called Tim—woke from his slumber and purred as he stretched and yawned. When not in the middle of an active investigation, Tim tended to hide in the recesses of PJ's brain, though he was never too far away to be called upon. PJ was still figuring out the extent of Tim's abilities, having only learned of them in the past month, and one of the most useful was that the dragon could extend his senses farther than PJ could, giving him a bird's-eye (or dragon's-eye, as it were) view of the world while his physical body stayed put.

PJ's eyes burned as Tim took over, and the colors of the world inverted from greens to purple and blues to green. In PJ's mind, the dragon took flight, rising higher above the two boys on the ground, scanning the horizon.

"There's definitely a village," PJ said, as Tim drew as close as he was able to the collection of buildings. "And a gigantic mansion next door. Wonder what that's about?"

Tim swept above the small town, with only a few non-vacant shopfronts and a two-story inn. It seemed in need of some upkeep but didn't strike PJ as too terribly frightening—especially as someone walked out of the inn.

"I think we're good. Definitely people there."

But as he said that, Tim rose once more, casting his dragon's gaze on the gigantic forest a stone's throw from the inn—a forest he could see bits and pieces of as the dragon but that seemed to be covered in a thick veil of magic. Something about it sent shivers down his human spine, and he snapped back into himself, blinking away the magic.

"What?" Grant asked.

"N-Nothing," PJ said, forcing a smile. "Shall we? I'm starving."

~

The road to the village led them by the mansion, which was even larger and more intimidating up close. It was at least four levels, constructed with bricks that had been painted white, with black shutters hanging on either side of the windows. A tall wrought iron gate cordoned off the premises, and PJ gave it wide berth, as iron and magic didn't mix. But Grant couldn't help his curiosity, walking up to the fence and peering through the gaps.

"Imagine what it would be like to live in a place like that, eh?" Grant said. "I'd probably sleep in a different bed every night. 'Oh, tonight I'll sleep in the green room.' 'Oh, tonight, I'm feeling the red curtained room.'" He clapped his hands together excitedly.

"I'd hate to be the servant who had to change your sheets every night," PJ said. "Having to look in twenty rooms just to find where you felt like crashing."

"I mean, I'd tell 'em where I'd been sleeping. If only so they'd know where to bring me breakfast in bed." He flashed PJ a mischievous grin. "Yeah, I think I'd be great at being rich." His smile faded, as perhaps he recalled that, for a very brief moment, he *had* been rich.

Before they'd begun their quest, Grant had been in line to inherit a small fortune—not a sum that would've allowed him to purchase a property this size but enough to set him up for a few years in Sheepsburg. The only requirement for him to access this money was that he complete his university studies—and while he was in school, his tuition and apartment would be fully paid for. Grant's sister had asked PJ to come along, partially to give him an opportunity he wouldn't get elsewhere, but also because Vicky knew Grant needed babysitting. But PJ's influence hadn't been enough, and Grant's grades had slipped beyond the point of no return. Just as they'd been facing eviction, a letter had arrived from the grannies, along with PJ's new amulet, and they'd been on a journey to find more dragon shifters like PJ ever since.

"Hey! You!" a gruff voice called. "Get outta here!"

Grant jumped away from the fence as if someone had zapped him with a spell. A very old, very grizzled man burst from the bushes near the house, carrying a garden rake like a weapon. He thrust it toward Grant, who was still safely on the other side of the fence, and snarled.

"Get off the property!" he barked.

"Whoa, friend," Grant said, holding up his hands in surrender. "I'm not doing any harm. I'm just looking."

"Take your eyeballs somewhere else then!" He shook the rake threateningly. "I know how it is with you highway bandits. You start by lookin', then you get a bit braver and start wanderin'. Next thing we know, all the silver's been stolen!"

"I'm not interested in—"

"Grant, let's leave this fine gentleman alone," PJ said, taking his friend by the shoulder and pulling him away. "We're just passing by. Apologies for the disruption."

"Just make sure you keep on passin'," he said, setting the rake upright next to him and watching them hawkishly.

The boys walked briskly away, PJ feeling the angry man's gaze for the duration of the walk. He half-expected the man to follow them into the small town, just to make sure they kept moving, but he remained safely behind the iron fence.

Grant let out a breath once they made it into the village, shivering and shaking his head. "On second thought, if that's what having a house that size turns you into, I don't think I want one."

"I don't think he's the owner," PJ said mildly. "Probably just the gardener. I don't think he'd be carrying a rake otherwise."

"True." Grant turned to inspect the town. "Not much to Cheshireville, is there?"

It might've been one of the tiniest towns PJ had ever seen. There was the inn, plus a bakery, a butcher shop, a cidery, a launderer (oddly enough), and…that was about it.

"Well, suppose that's why there's that sign back at the main road," Grant said with a shrug. "Though I wonder how many prospective customers are run off by Angry McSourpuss before they even find the town?"

"Oh, did you run into Harold?" a voice asked from behind them. Two men stood in front of the launderer, one tall with short gray hair and the other stockier, with a red tinge to his gray. By their clothes, it was clear they'd been traveling, although they didn't carry any bags.

Grant nodded. "He was gonna run me through with his rake just for standing too close to his fence."

"He's the groundskeeper there," the taller one said. "He used to be a little better, but now in his old age… And he definitely doesn't like strangers."

"Suppose you boys aren't from around here," the shorter one said with a kind smile. "All of us regulars know it's best to give Thornhill Manor a wide berth when approaching Cheshireville, lest you run afoul of the terrifying gardener." He pointed to himself. "I'm Roe McKeown. This is my brother Oscar."

The boys introduced themselves. "Do you two live here?" PJ asked.

Roe shook his head. "We're traveling merchants. But we do a lot of business between Merrittville and Caldona, and this spot is exactly halfway between them, so we're about as local as you can get without actually living here."

"What are you two doing in town?" Oscar asked. "Just passing through?"

PJ nodded, but Grant puffed out his chest. "We're magical investigators. We hear there's a forest nearby where some folks hid out from the queen. We thought we'd stop in and see if there are any problems that need solving."

"Oh, yeah." Roe thumbed toward the looming tree line in the distance. "Over there. But it's mostly empty now. Not going to find much of anything exciting."

Oscar nodded fervently. "And the rest of this town is just this. A couple folks who used to support Thornhill Manor, but who rely on that lovely inn and travelers to keep their businesses afloat."

"Used to support?" PJ asked.

"The previous Master Thornhill—Marley—was a big magical merchant. Used to throw all kinds of parties for his wizard friends. Of course, all that ended when the queen's folks showed up," Roe said.

PJ could only imagine. "So the manor's empty now?"

"Marley Thornhill's son Ellison still lives there—lucky guy got spared by the queen since he wasn't actually involved in magical stuff—but he hasn't thrown a party in…ever. Too bookish, you know?" Roe continued. "So the town was dying until Kishan started the inn. It's not as prosperous as it was, but at least no one had to leave. Kishan put that sign at the crossroads, too, which encourages people to take a chance on us."

"It caught our attention," Grant said. "Though he may want to refresh the paint or something. Looks like a sign for an abandoned town."

"You can tell him when you meet him," Oscar said with a laugh. "C'mon. We'll introduce you."

The boys turned to follow the merchants toward the inn, but PJ stumbled over his feet as a chill ran down his spine.

He blinked, his gaze landing on something dark moving in the magical forest. A very distinct shadow as tall as the trees it moved through. When its eyes met PJ's, the chill turned into an all-out shudder that made his teeth chatter.

But a moment later, the shadow was gone. No matter how long PJ searched, he couldn't find it anywhere.

"Did you see that, Tim?" PJ asked, his voice low.

Yes. Odd.

"Not a dragon, though, right?" PJ said, unsure why the sight had unnerved him.

Probably not.

"Probably isn't definitive," PJ said uneasily.

"Oi!" Grant called, snapping PJ from his reverie. He stood at the front door to the inn. "Peej. Did you fall asleep over there?"

"I'm c-coming," PJ said, the sensation still making his heart flutter.

Grant seemed to sense PJ was off and jogged over. "What's up? Did Tim sense something?"

The good thing about Grant was that PJ could tell him just about anything, and Grant would just listen, nod, and accept that whatever PJ was saying was true—especially if Tim was in agreement about it.

"I've never felt anything like that before," PJ said.

"Could it be a dragon?"

"Tim doesn't think so," PJ said. "It was... strange, that's for sure."

"I mean, if it's *probably* not a dragon, maybe we can just...not go there?" Grant said with trepidation. "Let it be? Monsters are allowed to live in peace if they aren't bothering anyone, aren't they?"

"Suppose you're right," PJ said, feeling a *little* bit better that Grant's logic was solid enough to give him an excuse not to investigate further. Fear hadn't been too common on this journey, and something about that forest was setting off warning bells in his mind. "Unless there's a problem, we'll let it be. Let's just get our room and a square meal, and find out where the next closest town is."

"Already ahead of you."

CHAPTER TWO

The inn was warm and welcoming, and the innkeeper smiled as Grant brought PJ over. He was middle-aged, with a charming smile, pale skin, and brown hair cut short against his scalp.

"Good evening," he said, his voice a soothing baritone. "Welcome to the Cheshireville Inn. Your friend tells me you'd like to rent a room? That'll be one gold coin."

PJ reached into his pocket and pulled out the gold coin, drawn from a dragon's hoard somewhere far away, that his amulet had deposited there with a *thump*. "You have a lovely place here."

"It's a quiet town, but we do have a steady

stream of visitors," he said, scribbling down the information Grant had presumably given him in his small book. "I've seen Roe and Oscar at least four times in the past three weeks. But I think it's Adonna's custards that keep bringing them back."

"Custards?" PJ asked.

"You'll have to ask them about it," Kishan said with a smile. "Will you be staying one night?"

"As of right now, yes, but..." PJ shared a look with Grant. "I had a question about the forest. We heard there was a magical enclave in there. Is anyone still living there?"

And are they anywhere near that giant shadow I just saw?

"Not as many as there were before, I suspect," Kishan said. "When the queen fell, a stream of creatures paraded out, but I hear some remained."

"We've met a few folks from there," PJ said. "Ogres."

"Oh yeah, there were all kinds. Ogres, witches, gnomes, elves, centaurs, you name it," he said. "I think most of 'em went back to their old towns and lives, but you've still got a handful of folks living there." He handed PJ a key. "Dinner's almost ready, so feel free to drop your things off and come down. Anything else I can help you with?"

"Just one more question," PJ said, hoping he didn't regret asking. "Was there a giant monster-like thing living in this enclave?"

A shadow fell across the innkeeper's face. "What?"

"I thought I saw a shadow in the forest. It was huge—maybe the size of a house. It could've been my eyes playing tricks on me, but—"

"There's no *monster*." A voice echoed from behind them. A young man, perhaps five or six years older than PJ and Grant, with brown skin and curly hair that hung in perfect ringlets around his face, walked in from the kitchen, holding a crate in both arms. "I don't know what you've heard, but—"

"I didn't hear it," PJ said abruptly. "I saw it. Just now, as I was walking inside."

The young man opened and closed his mouth, some of the color draining from his face.

"What's he talking about, Ellison?" Kishan asked.

"Ellison as in the rich guy who owns that big house?" Grant asked, suddenly more interested. "Nice to meet you. I'm Grant, this is PJ. We met your gardener. Your house is great. I'd love to see it."

But Ellison wasn't listening to Grant. "I, erm. I'm sure you saw nothing. The forest is strange— magical, you know. Sometimes you think you see things, and you really don't." He cleared his throat. "What are you two doing in town, hm?"

"They're *magical investigators*," Roe said from

one of the tables. "Got any magical problems you need them to solve?"

Ellison surveyed PJ and Grant. "You don't look too much like magical investigators. Why have you come to Cheshireville?"

"We were passing by and found the sign," PJ said. "It was getting late, and we were just planning on spending the night and moving on. But then I saw that…thing in the forest." He did his best not to shudder. "And I was curious about it."

"Oh, it was probably just your imagination," Ellison said, casting a nervous glance toward Kishan and the two merchants. "There's nothing wrong in Forest Den. In fact, we're happier than ever!"

"Then why did I see a family of elves leaving earlier this morning?" Kishan asked with a raised brow. "And a pair of witches left a week ago?"

"They were, erm, ready to move on." Ellison shifted. "Were there any more crates of potatoes in today's delivery, Kishan?"

Kishan shook his head. "I took what I ordered. Whatever's left is what you ordered."

"Very well." Ellison looked put out but didn't argue. "Have a good night—"

"Wait," PJ said, taking a step forward, sensing his voice was more Tim's than his own. "Is it possible for us to go to the enclave?"

Ellison and Grant blanched at the same time,

and came out with a unanimous, "*Why?*"

PJ asked Tim the same question, though silently. *Shouldn't we just leave well enough alone?*

You dragon. Stop worry.

PJ licked his lips as the dragon receded into his mind once more. He didn't deny something fishy seemed to be happening around here—Ellison's adamant claim that PJ hadn't seen anything, Kishan's comment about people leaving... Even Ellison's conversation with Kishan seemed off, like there was something to uncover.

"I've heard a lot about it," PJ said after a long pause. It was the only thing he could say that was somewhat close to the truth. "Thought it might be interesting to see." He turned to Grant, who was eyeing him curiously. "We can stop in first thing, then be on our way to the next town."

Ellison seemed on the verge of arguing then clearly thought better of it. "In the morning, I'd be...*happy* to take you. Just for a quick visit." He glanced at Kishan. "If you find you don't use all those potatoes, please let me know."

~

Ellison left shortly after that, and PJ went upstairs to deposit their things, as Grant had already found the cask of cider and had gotten into a conversation with the merchants. PJ dropped his bag on the bed closest to the window and stared out at the forest beyond. Magic tingled his senses, even from this distance, but he didn't spot any more moving shadows.

Had Tim been seeing things, too?

I don't mistake.

"So sorry," PJ said with a chuckle. He'd gotten into hot water with his mental dragon back in Padstow for being too loose with his abilities, and he wanted to avoid another period of Tim not speaking to him. "I just… What we saw was so big. It's hard to believe everyone doesn't know about it."

Rich human hide something. Should find out what.

"Do we have to?" PJ muttered, looking around. "I mean, is it our business?"

Thwap.

Tim's tail smacked hard against the walls of PJ's mind, reminding PJ just how ornery his dragon could be. "Fine. We'll go. But if we don't find anything…"

When PJ returned downstairs, dinner was in full swing. Grant had ingratiated himself with Roe and Oscar, of course, but they'd been joined by another four people. Grant had made PJ a plate of food and saved him a seat, and PJ gratefully took both with a smile.

"I was just meeting the townsfolk," Grant explained. "That's Adonna, the baker," he started, pointing at the woman seated next to him. "She's the one who makes the delicious custards Roe and Oscar were raving about."

"You'll have to stop in tomorrow," she said with a kind smile. "I also made the bread that accompanied tonight's dinner."

"Brennan is the cider maker," Grant said. "This is his brew." He tapped the tankard. "It's outstanding."

PJ took a tentative sip, waiting for sweetness but instead getting a unique blend of tart and alcohol. "That's delicious."

Brennan beamed. "You'll have to tell your friends. Bring them to our small town."

"What? We're not doing our best?" Roe said with a mock gasp. "Look at all the people we've brought!" He gestured to the empty table next to them.

The rest of the diners, save PJ and Grant, chuckled at the joke, as if they were used to this sort of quip.

"I'm Ulysses. I own the butcher shop across the way," said a large man with a handlebar mustache. He pointed to the round-cheeked, rosy-faced woman next to him. "This is Orlena, my wife. She runs the laundry shop."

"I was curious about that," PJ said. "It's probably a quiet business without many people around."

It seemed to be the wrong question, as everyone at the table bristled. "It wasn't a bad business, when there were twenty beds to change every night," she said, a little ruefully.

"Ah, that's right, you said Thornhill Manor used to have lots of parties, right?" Grant said. "And then the queen came through and no more parties?"

"It's more that Ellison Thornhill took over his father's mansion, and he's such a pretentious little bookworm that he probably doesn't know the first meaning of the word 'friend,'" Ulysses said with a glower.

"Why haven't you left, then?" Grant asked.

"A lot of us did," Brennan said. "But thanks to Kishan's inn, those of us who couldn't bear to leave our small town behind have some relief." He thumbed toward the kitchen, where the innkeeper had presumably already started on the dishes. "It may not look like it today, but we do have a pretty steady line of customers in the summer and around the winter solstice. Folks who just need a night to rest their heads on their long journeys."

"Besides the fact he pays us handsomely, he's always talking us up to the people who pass through," Ulysses said. "The missus here offers a clothes-washing service to the folks who stay at the inn, in addition to having a contract with Kishan."

"I sell my casks to the inn, and Kishan helped me reach some of the larger towns," Brennan said. "And he's helped Adonna's bakery, too."

She nodded. "This past summer, I baked no fewer than twenty solstice pies. It was my best year yet!"

"All thanks to Kishan," Orlena said with a bright smile. "Without him, we'd be sunk."

PJ smiled. "We had an innkeeper back in Pigsend who was kinda like that. She helped everyone she could. One of the best people you could ever meet."

"Are you lot talking too good about me again?" Kishan said, walking out of the kitchen with another plate of sliced bread. "Don't listen to a word they say. I'm a cad."

Based on the looks of admiration from the rest of the town, that clearly wasn't their opinion.

"Are all of you from here?" Grant asked.

They all nodded. "I used to work at Thornhill Manor as a manservant," Brennan said. "Took over the cidery after Ellison canned me."

"And I was the in-house baker before," Adonna said. "Of course, Ellison didn't see the need to keep one on, so he fired me, too."

"I take it you two worked at the house, too?" PJ asked the married couple.

They nodded. "Everyone who lived in

Cheshireville worked there," Ulysses said.

"What about you, Kishan?" PJ asked.

"I was a traveling entertainer," the innkeeper said with a thin smile. "When the queen's folks took over, I decided to put down roots here and start the inn. Just lucky there was a building here already, though I had to put in some elbow grease to set it up." To Grant's curious look, he added, "I performed at Thornhill Manor at least once a month, so I was familiar with the town."

"So the queen's people took over, Ellison inherited that big mansion, and he fired all his father's workers?" Grant asked, tapping his chin. "Did he replace them with anyone?"

Adonna shook her head. "The only person who still works there is Harold."

"Oh, the gardener." PJ grimaced. "We met him."

"I don't think he'd leave even if Ellison did fire him," Brennan said with a chuckle. "He's rather protective of his plants and grounds. And maybe Ellison kept him on because he didn't want to have to toil away. But he sure didn't keep anyone else around."

"Not even a launderer?" PJ asked. "Does he wash his own bedsheets?"

Orlena gave a disgusted face. "I'm sure I don't know, and I don't care. He burned his bridge when he fired us without warning."

PJ turned to Kishan. "Why was he at the inn earlier today?"

Kishan cleared his throat. "He was picking up his half of our weekly shipment. And he usually gets a bite to eat in the kitchen if he hasn't already fed himself. As you can probably imagine, it's a bit tense if he's here when everyone else is."

"I wish that—" Adonna began, but the front door burst open.

Harold, wearing the same dirt-covered clothes PJ and Grant had seen him in earlier, limped inside, glowering at everyone at the table, spending an extra few seconds on PJ and Grant before continuing to the remnants of dinner. He piled his plate without a word then shuffled toward the empty table, sitting down with a loud clang and digging in.

"Have a good day, Harold?" Orlena offered with a too-bright smile.

"Better if I wasn't breakin' bread with these scavengers," he snarled, nodding toward PJ and Grant.

"We're just staying the night," Grant said. "Promise, we have no interest in your silver or whatever else you have in that big mansion."

"So you say." He turned to PJ with an appraising look. "I hear you saw the typhon."

"The..." PJ and Grant shared a look. "The

what?"

The old man chuckled as he aggressively cut a potato. "The typhon. As tall as the trees, with hands so strong they could crush a pipsqueak like you without a second look. It lives in the forest. Only shows itself to interlopers who're up to no good." He smirked as PJ swallowed involuntarily. "Seems like it's coming for *you* tonight, son."

PJ recalled the way his whole body had shivered, the sensation of something not quite right in his gut. The size of it.

You dragon. Stop worry.

Tim's voice rang clearly in PJ's mind, halting the fear before it gripped him and bringing him back to the here and now.

"If it does, we'll be happy to handle it," Grant answered smoothly. "We may look young, but we've got a few tricks up our sleeve."

"Oh, Harold, you threaten every single traveler who comes through here with this typhon nonsense," Adonna said with a hearty eye roll.

"Just an old wives' tale from the forest." Ulysses shook his bald head. "Don't you two worry about it. If there was a monster like that lurking around in the trees, wouldn't those magical folks have seen it?"

But Harold kept PJ's gaze, perhaps knowing that PJ *had* seen something and wanting to drive home the point. "Lots of interesting stuff happening in there lately. You've seen the magical folks streaming out in droves. They're scared of something, I tell ya, and from what I heard, it sounds like a typhon. You two had best be on your way *first thing* in the morning. Don't want the creature getting any ideas and coming to rampage out here."

"Enough, Harold," Kishan said with a sideways look. "You've been treading on thin ice for weeks now. If you keep trying to scare off my customers, I'm gonna ban you from the dining room. Understand?"

The old man slid his withering glare from PJ to Kishan. Then, as if deciding it wasn't worth it, he snorted and turned back to his food.

Adonna smiled apologetically as she patted Grant's hand. "Ignore him. He's always trying to stir up trouble."

"It's all well and good for him to scare off potential customers," Orlena huffed, her voice loud and seeming not to care that Harold was still in the room. "He's still getting his monthly pay. Doesn't have to worry about customers at all, does he?"

"You said there were still folks in the forest, right?" PJ asked. "Surely, they're providing you some business, right?"

Disdain rippled through the room. "Not really," Ulysses said with a frown.

"They have everything they need, it seems,"

Orlena replied with a sigh. "And they've been quite insular in their little enclave."

"We tried to go in," Brennan explained. "But the forest wouldn't let us—"

"And rightfully so!" Harold interjected. "That forest is full of things that would sooner eat you than shake your hand. Ain't nobody needs to be going in there—nor *living* there, neither." He pointed at PJ and Grant again. "You two'll find out tomorrow when you go. If the forest even lets you in." He cracked a wry smile. "You might not be getting out."

"Harold, *seriously*," Kishan said with an exasperated sigh. "Knock it off."

Harold just shrugged, smirking to himself like he knew what was going to happen the next day. And PJ couldn't help but feel like the old man just might.

CHAPTER THREE

"What do you make of that?" Grant asked as the boys settled into bed. "I'm leaning toward 'angry old man wants to scare us out of town,' but…"

"I definitely saw something that fits his description," PJ said, staring at the wooden ceiling. "Something I've never seen before. It was big and terrifying. I certainly wouldn't want to meet that in a dark forest."

"*You're* big and terrifying," Grant replied. "You could shift into dragon form and go toe to toe— well, claw-to-claw?—with that giant if you had a mind to."

PJ snorted, remembering Tim's chiding earlier.

"Just one problem with that. I'm not supposed to shift without the grannies nearby."

"Right, right," Grant said, as if that were a minor inconvenience. "But don't forget, you can also spit fire when you want to, eh? And who knows what else Tim has up his sleeve? Seems like there's a new skill every day with him."

"Yes, but you didn't see what I did, Grant," PJ said. "It was *exactly* like Harold described."

Grant sniffed. "I'm taking everything Grumpy Grandpa says with a grain of salt. We'll just see what the citizens of that forest enclave have to say. I'm sure they'll be happy to tell us what's really going on."

"Something tells me we're here for the long haul," PJ said.

"Well, I won't be mad about it. Dinner was delicious. And that cider..." Grant sighed. "Night, Peej."

PJ slept fitfully, his dreams plagued by a massive shadow moving through the forest and watching him with red eyes—eyes that looked similar to his own, somehow. It roared as loudly as a dragon then pushed away trees as it ran toward him—

No.

Tim's voice stopped PJ's dreams in its tracks. He blinked in the early morning sunlight, the sound of a loud bird chirping outside the window replacing the echoes of roaring in his mind. He sat up, wiping his sweaty face, and pressed his palm to his chest, where his heart beat wildly. Across the room, Grant was still snoring, a thin line of drool puddling on his pillow.

Human silly. No fear typhon. Dragon more powerful.

"I'm so sorry I'm a silly human," PJ said, annoyance seeping into his voice. "But whatever that thing was spooked me. And the old man's stories didn't help, either."

At PJ's voice, Grant woke abruptly, rubbing his face. "Wha? Is it time? Who're you talking to?"

"Tim."

"Oh." Grant rolled over to face away from PJ. "What's he say?"

PJ honestly didn't want to share it. On some level, he knew Tim was right. He was a powerful dragon with enough magic to destroy a magical forest—as he'd done in Gilramore. But...

Grant's snores echoed once more, and PJ actually found them soothing.

"You know, you're lucky you don't have voices in your head telling you what to do," PJ said, standing and walking to the window. He once again searched the forest for anything suspicious but found nothing other than birds flying to and from the trees.

"It's just trees and woods and maybe a little magic," PJ muttered to himself. "Nothing to get bent out of shape about. We can handle this."

Yes, came Tim's deep voice.

~

At eight o'clock, Ellison came by the inn to take PJ and Grant to the village. He gave Kishan a cursory nod, almost avoiding his gaze, and beckoned PJ and Grant to follow him. He didn't seem to stop twitching until the trio were out of the cluster of buildings that comprised the village, walking the grassy fields toward the imposing forest.

"Do you think the forest will let us in?" Grant asked.

Ellison gave him a double take. "What do you mean?"

Grant told him what the others had said the night before about the forest not letting them in.

Ellison let out a small chuckle. "They didn't… What happened isn't what they thought. You're with me. You'll be let in."

"So how did this town come to be?" Grant asked. "Did someone invite all the magical folks here, or…?"

"It really was by accident," Ellison said. "When the queen's soldiers came through, all the magical creatures fled. Some of them kept running, but others, drawn by the magic, came to the forest just to hide. The forest, being what it is, made a clearing, created houses, that sort of thing. It's like it knew that all these magical people needed a safe place to land."

"It created houses?" PJ said.

"You'll see," Ellison said. "It also made sure the queen's folks never made it too far. They kept coming, promising they were going to burn the forest down, but it wouldn't catch fire." He chuckled. "After a few attempts, I think they realized they were outmatched, so they left it alone."

"Did the same thing happen to the townsfolk in Cheshireville when they tried to walk in?" Grant asked.

"They had ulterior motives," Ellison said abruptly, clearly not wanting to continue that conversation. "In any case, you two said you were magical investigators. If you're willing, I'd like to hire you."

PJ and Grant shared a look of surprise. "Really? What's going on?" Grant asked.

"About three weeks ago, the residents were rudely awoken by a loud roar and the earth shaking. Like something monstrous was walking around the clearing."

PJ swallowed, grateful Ellison had turned away so he wouldn't see the fear that surely flitted across his face. Tim's low growl echoed in his mind, and PJ did his best to quell his nerves.

"So there is a typhon, then," Grant said, finally sounding a little nervous.

"That's the thing—nobody's actually *seen* anything," Ellison said with an exasperated breath. "It's been a lot of loud ruckus in the middle of the night, so they tell me. It was enough to scare half the town into packing up and leaving after that first time, I'll tell you that much. And those who stayed keep acting like they're going to leave if it keeps happening."

"So what do you want us to do about it?" PJ asked.

"I'd like you to look into it, figure out if it's actually something to be worried about, or if the forest is just being...the forest." Ellison nodded toward the imposing tree line ahead of them. "And, more than anything, put the citizens of Forest Den at ease."

"Why didn't you want to mention any of this to the folks back there?" Grant asked, thumbing back toward the small town behind them. "You told us flat-out there wasn't a monster. Didn't want Kishan to know about it, either."

"The townsfolk are already very distrustful of the forest," Ellison said.

"And hate you, too," Grant pointed out.

Ellison turned, his cheeks darkening. "Look, it's

frankly none of their business what happens in the forest. But I'd rather they not spread nasty rumors. I just want whatever is happening to stop. For the people of Forest Den to feel safe."

"Why?" Grant asked.

Based on the tension in his shoulders and the strain in his voice, Ellison was scrambling for something to say other than the truth. "It's their home. They've already suffered enough, being treated the way they were by the queen. And it's just… It seems rather…" He cleared his throat. "Anyway. You wanted to look around. So you can look around. And maybe you can tell me if there's really something to be worried about."

PJ and Grant shared a knowing glance but kept any further questions to themselves. Ellison hastened his pace toward the forest, and as they drew closer, magic pressed in on PJ's skin. It was similar to the magical forest back in Gilramore, except on a much larger scale, like comparing a glass of water to the ocean.

You dragon came Tim's ever-present reminder.

But as soon as PJ crossed under the shadow of the first tree, his dragon grew silent. PJ stopped suddenly, mentally searching for the presence that had been his constant companion and came back with nothing.

"Peej?" Grant asked.

"One moment," PJ said, taking four steps back until he was out of the forest. "Tim?"

Magic strong. Muddle talking.

"I thought you said I was a dragon," PJ muttered, casting his gaze up at the trees.

You still dragon. Just restrained dragon. Go in.

PJ didn't like the sound of that, but he also didn't want to lose his guide or Grant, so he swallowed his nerves and marched back into the forest. As before, Tim went silent, and there was quiet in his mind for the first time in weeks. Even when Tim hadn't been speaking to him, PJ had always felt his presence. Now, it was the same as when he'd had his first amulet, when his magic had been completely dampened to the point of nonexistence.

It was, if possible, more unnerving than seeing a gigantic monster.

"What's up?" Grant asked when PJ fell into step behind him.

"This forest is chock full of magic," he said, barely above a whisper. "It's interfering with my connection to Tim."

Grant let out a breath. "What does that mean? You don't have any super special dragon powers?"

"Not at the moment, no," PJ muttered, looking around. "Hope that means there isn't a giant on its way to grind my bones or whatever else Harold said."

"What's going on back there?" Ellison asked, turning to PJ and Grant.

"Peej is just having a bit of trouble with his—" Grant began but PJ cut him off.

"It's nothing," he said. "We're following."

Ellison eyed him. "You're magical, aren't you?" It wasn't a question.

PJ nodded. "The forest is doing funny things to me."

Ellison nodded in understanding. "The forest probably doesn't trust you yet…erm, what was your name again?"

"PJ." He craned his neck, looking at the trees and forest around him. "How do I get a forest to trust me?"

"Well, you could start by telling it what you are and why you're here." Ellison watched the trees, and his tone was neutral, as if he were trying to sort through the answer himself.

"You seem to know a lot about this forest," Grant said.

"I've spent a lot of time here," Ellison said. "I'm not as good as Ingrid, but… You'll meet Ingrid when we get inside the enclave."

"Is this why the Cheshireville townsfolk weren't allowed inside?" Grant asked. "Because the forest didn't trust them?"

"Mm." Ellison nodded to PJ. "Well?"

PJ took a few steps forward, breathing in the earthy scents of the woods and underbrush. He knelt, touching the dead leaves and sensing the magic even in that. He searched for Tim but came back with nothing.

"My name is PJ Norris," he began softly, so only the forest would hear. "I'm a dragon shifter looking for more of my kind. Ellison invited my friend Grant and me to Forest Den to investigate the mysterious noises. I'm not here to cause trouble. I just want to help."

The dead leaves rustled under his fingertips, then some of the pressure eased from his chest. The forest grew brighter, too, like the sun had just come out from behind clouds. And more importantly, twenty steps ahead, where dense, thick forest had been, there lay a clear path.

"I guess it trusts us now," Grant said, perhaps seeing the same difference.

Ellison smiled, almost looking relieved. "Wonderful."

"Tim?" PJ muttered, listening for his dragon. "Are you there?"

Nothing. So the forest trusted him a *little*, but not enough to fully have access to his dragon.

That wouldn't cause problems or anything.

"Are you okay?" Grant asked, perhaps reading

the discomfort on PJ's face.

"Y-yeah, I'm…"

Movement caught PJ's attention and he whipped his head around to scan the trees for any sign of the shadow he'd seen. A bird chirped nearby and he nearly jumped out of his skin.

"Just a bird, tough guy," Grant said, grabbing PJ before he toppled over. "What's happening? What does Tim say?"

"Tim's not available at the moment," PJ said.

His heart pounded in his ears—*thump, thump, thump*—or was that the creature, walking toward him? He turned again, looking wildly around in search of the sounds he was *sure* he was hearing. Was that the creature, or was it the sun just streaming in through the treetops? Was that the creature? Or a bird flapping its wings? He truly couldn't tell reality from his mind playing tricks on him.

"Tim?" he whispered hastily. "If you're here…"

But, of course, the dragon was nowhere to be found. He was truly on his own—a mere human facing—

"Peej?"

PJ turned abruptly, finding Grant and Ellison staring at him curiously. Neither one of them had heard the monster approaching, nor did they seem concerned in the least.

"You didn't hear that?" PJ said, again, looking

around. "You don't s-see anything?"

Ellison frowned, looking around. "What am I supposed to be looking for?"

PJ clutched his chest. Could only magical folks sense the monster? What he wouldn't do for Tim's deep voice to set him straight. What was he supposed to do if he couldn't reach his monster?

He glanced behind him, looking longingly for the edge of the forest. If he left, he'd surely be able to speak to Tim and get some answers. But the forest behind him was thick and repetitive, and if Ellison hadn't been leading the way, he'd surely have been lost. That, too, made panic spiral in his bones. What were they to do if their guide disappeared? What would happen if—

PJ jumped at the touch of Grant's hand on his shoulder. "You good?" he asked, concern evident in his gaze.

"You really don't hear anything?" PJ could've sworn he could still hear *thump, thump, thump* somewhere, but he saw nothing. Not even a ripple in the air that might reveal something hidden in plain sight. "What if it's only visible to magical people? Or dragons? I don't know anything about typhons. Do they have invisibility or super speed or anything like that?"

"Say, Ellison?" Grant began, raising his voice. "About this monster..."

"What about it?" Ellison asked, casting a nervous look around.

"You said nobody's seen it, right?" Grant asked, his hand still firmly on PJ's shoulder, grounding him to the moment.

"Yes," he said. "But we've all heard it."

Grant smirked. "Ellison, do you hear the monster now?"

Ellison jumped, looking around. "N-no. No, I don't. And it was unmistakable. The loudest roar, sounding like a creature that could eat you whole. Absolutely terrifying. Chilled you right to the bone."

"Peej, what are you hearing?" Grant asked. "*Really* hearing?"

PJ swallowed hard, holding fast to the tether of relation of his best friend's hand. *Thump, thump, thump*—that was, in fact, PJ's rapid pulse, not a creature walking toward him. The rustling of the trees was just the wind. And when he quieted the racing thoughts in his human mind, he got the sense that there was nothing to be worried about.

"Is there something I should know?" Ellison asked, watching the two of them between furtive looks toward the canopy.

"Nope," PJ said with a firm nod to Grant, who removed his hand. "No, sorry. The magic is messing with me, I think. But we're good to continue."

"Mm." Ellison eyed him. "Very well. It's just up ahead." He turned and kept walking through the trees.

Grant hung back to walk with PJ. "What was that?"

"Not sure," PJ said. "But I don't think it's the last time the forest is going to confuse me."

CHAPTER FOUR

They walked for about half an hour, Ellison following some unseen path, and thankfully, PJ avoided any more panicked moments. He was still shaky, still unsure of what he was hearing and seeing, but he kept his focus on Ellison. If the manor owner wasn't sensing anything, there was nothing to worry about.

Finally, they came to what PJ assumed was Forest Den. There were gigantic trees, thicker than anything PJ had ever seen before, with trunks that reached higher than the tallest buildings, before disappearing into the green canopy far above them. These trees were also homes, boasting front doors painted in cheery pinks, yellows, and blues, along with windows and floral boxes overflowing with late-season flowers. The stepping-stone paths between the homes were well-worn, surrounded by soft, verdant moss. Mushrooms of all shapes and sizes dotted the landscape, including a rather unique collection that resembled a dining room with large, flat caps surrounded by smaller white puffs.

One of the doors opened and a man stepped out —PJ had to stop himself before doing a double take. The man was bare-chested, with pale skin and long, flowing hair that came down to his...very horse-like bottom half. Indeed, he had four legs with hooves. Not that PJ would ask the man, who seemed brawny and stern as Ellison flagged him down.

"Morning, Bill," he said. "Have you seen Ingrid?"

"She's dealing with a small problem over at Melinda's," Bill said. "One of the trees got confused and ate her reading chair."

"Dear me, that does seem to be happening a lot lately, doesn't it?" Ellison said with a click of his tongue.

"Not any more than usual. Ingrid'll sort it," he said, eyeing the two new people. "Who's this?"

"I've, erm, hired them to investigate these strange noises happening at night," Ellison said. "Was hoping Ingrid could escort them out into the forest. I'd do it, but she's able to get farther than I can. Besides that, the shipment of goods last night was only half of what I ordered, so I've got head back to town to get the rest of it."

Bill nodded in understanding. "I'm running low on nails, by the way. If you're able to put in another order."

Ellison winced. "Erm, really? I thought I just bought you a box last week?"

"Yes, and you asked me to build a lot of furniture," Bill said, folding his muscly arms over his chest. "Furniture takes nails—"

"Yes, yes." Ellison sighed. "I'll…see what I can do." He turned to PJ and Grant. "I'm going to leave you with Bill until Ingrid gets back. I hope to return sometime this afternoon." His gaze lingered on PJ, as if thinking about the way he'd nearly lost his marbles earlier. "Good luck. I do hope you can sort this out for us."

With that, he turned and walked right back the way they'd come, disappearing into the forest within moments. Bill, PJ, and Grant stood around, looking at each other before Grant held out his hand.

"Grant Hamblin, and this is my associate, PJ Norris," he said. "What kinda creature are you?"

PJ slapped his hand to his forehead. "Grant…"

Bill chuckled, taking Grant's hand and shaking it. "Bill. I'm the town carpenter. And, since you asked, a centaur. But I assume boys your age probably didn't see a lot of magical creatures growing up." He turned to PJ, narrowing his gaze. "You're something. What are you?"

"See, it's not rude to ask," Grant said to PJ.

"Dragon shifter," PJ said with a look at his friend. "We're traveling the country looking for more like me, and we stopped at the inn just outside of town. Ellison mentioned you folks had been plagued by some kind of monster lately?"

Bill nodded. "It's been about three weeks now. Happens in the dead of night, usually, when everyone's asleep. Loudest noise I've ever heard in my life. Sounds like something with big, sharp teeth that could rip you to shreds."

"Have you ever experienced anything like this before?" PJ asked, ignoring the shudder that ran through him.

"Never in the seven years we've lived here," Bill said. "But this forest is big and likes to hide things. It was great for us when we were kept safe from the queen, but now…"

"Ellison said no one's actually seen the thing, right?" Grant said. "And it hasn't caused any damage, other than scaring people."

"Not yet," Bill said. "But based on how it sounds, I'm sure it probably would if it decided to come into the village."

"We've got a theory it might be a typhon," PJ said. "Have you heard of it?"

Bill shook his head, frowning. "Never. But some of the other folks might've. Ingrid's been asking the forest, but it's not really telling her much about what's going on."

"Ellison's mentioned her," PJ said. "What kind of creature is she?"

"Dryad," Bill said. "She's our resident tree-communicator. She helps me find the wood for my projects."

PJ and Grant shared a curious look. "You aren't making anyone mad by chopping down their trees and stealing their flowers, right?" Grant asked.

Bill quirked a brow. "Erm. No. I'm only allowed to take what the forest gives me. Ingrid's real good about showing me the boundaries."

"Okay, mark that one off the list," Grant said to PJ with a sigh.

"What kind of projects do you do?" PJ asked. "You mentioned something about furniture?"

"Mr. Thornhill says he's working on something that'll help everyone in the village. He asked me to make furniture. I don't know any more than that."

PJ's brow furrowed. "Really? He didn't mention that to us."

"As I understand it, he's trying to keep things close to the vest until he's ready to reveal it," Bill said, looking like he might've already said too much.

PJ tucked that thought in the back of his mind to ask Ellison the next time they saw him. "Can you walk us through the last three weeks? Had anything changed before the monster showed up?"

Bill shook his head. "After the queen was overthrown, we'd had a big exodus of folks. Those who really wanted to get back to their homes, places of business, that sort of thing. But a lot of us really enjoyed living here, and it was even nicer with such a small community. Then, as I said, three weeks ago, the monster showed up. Scared about half the folks into leaving the next day—folks we really counted on to provide stuff."

"What do you mean?" PJ asked.

"Well, like our green witches," he said. "They were our apothecaries. Now Mr. Thornhill's got to purchase elixirs and tonics and the like and bring them here." He shook his head. "Poor guy's nearly out of money, too."

"You don't pay him?" Grant asked, sounding like that was the most horrible thing he'd ever heard in his life.

"It started off with him helping us because we were desperate," Bill said. "The queen being how she was, and all. Then, when she was gone, I don't know. We barter in here, of course, but it's not like we're generating a lot of gold for ourselves. Things we need outside of town… Well, Mr. Thornhill never said no to any of it."

"Interesting," PJ said, again putting that in the back of his mind. "Is this furniture building related to—"

"I really can't tell you much more than that I'm building it," he said. "Look, I'm behind schedule as it is. Got a late start. As soon as I see Ingrid, I'll be sure to send her your way. But for now—"

He slammed the door before PJ or Grant could say another word.

"Well, isn't this fun?" Grant said, putting his hands in his pockets. "Ellison's plotting something and now there's a monster trying to scare everyone out of town." He wagged his brow. "Smart money says Ellison's trying to clear the rest of the folks out so he can…I don't know. Sell the land?"

"He doesn't own it," PJ said, looking around and counting the tree-houses. Some seemed to lack the bright colors and decor of others. "And he said he didn't want anyone else to leave."

"Yeah, and people lie," Grant said. "You mean to tell me this rich man who lives in a gigantic house and fired all his workers has been paying for the food and supplies for a whole group of magical folks for *seven years* and never asked for anything in return?"

"I think we've been through this enough times

to know that someone being cagey doesn't always mean they're doing something unsavory," PJ said. "Our focus should be figuring out what this monster is and why it's suddenly showing up to terrorize the town." He couldn't help the look of uncertainty that crossed his face. "And hope it wants to clear out without any dragon-provided convincing."

"Easier said than done, I think," Grant said. "Well? Shall we venture into the forest in search of this monster? Or would you rather start knocking on doors?"

PJ was *not* actually keen on going back into the forest, so they walked up to the first tree house and rapped on the door. It swung open, and once again, PJ had to bite the inside of his cheek so he didn't gape at the strange creature in front of him. From the neck down, the man looked every bit the human, save the thick golden fur covering his body. But his head was very clearly a dog's, with floppy ears, a snout with a black nose, and a white muzzle.

And unlike Bill, he didn't seem bothered in the least that there were two strangers on his doorstep.

"Well, hi," he said, with an accent that drawled on the vowels. "Not usual for us to get strangers in our town, but glad to see some new faces." He tilted his head with a smile. "I'm Pat Lucky. Are you moving in?"

"N-no," PJ said, finally finding his tongue again,

as Grant still seemed to be thunderstruck. "Ellison hired us to look into the monster terrorizing you folks."

PJ hadn't noticed Pat's golden tail until it started wagging. "Oh, right-o. I tell ya, it's been a scary couple-a weeks here," he said, smiling like he was describing the weather and not like he was in any way worried about the monster. "We're just here, minding our business, then the roaring started. And I tell ya, half the town up and left that same day."

"But you didn't?" Grant asked.

"Yeah, it takes more than some loud noises to scare me," he said with a hearty chuckle. "Especially after Mr. Thornhill's been so nice to us."

PJ glanced at Grant, hoping he was thinking the same thing. This affable dog man seemed like he had lots of gossip to spill—and was eagerly doing so without reservation.

"What else can you tell us about what you've heard at night?" PJ asked, hoping he sounded innocent. "We'd like to get the measure of what we're dealing with before this evening."

"Oh, lots!" His tail wagged again. "Why don't you two come inside for a cuppa? I'll put on the kettle."

Pat led them into his tree house, which was a

single room that smelled very strongly of dog with a couch, bed, and small stove in the corner. There wasn't a single surface that hadn't been infused with Pat's golden fur, either. But otherwise, it seemed a cozy, welcoming space, and PJ and Grant gratefully took a seat on the couch while Pat tended to the kettle on the stove and regaled them with stories about the town during the queen's reign, about the personalities they might encounter, and a few more nice stories about Ellison bringing them everything he needed.

"So you've never left?" PJ asked. "Not even after the queen was overthrown?"

"Naw." Pat thought for a moment, and PJ could've sworn his ears twitched. "I mean, I could, I suppose. But we don't really want for much. Ellison still brings a wagonload of food and whatever else we need about once a week. He's bringing me some potatoes later for the town potluck."

"What's that?" Grant asked.

"We all gather around the old tavern—not much of a tavern now, since our barkeep left—but we all bring a dish or two to share. It's become a little tradition since the first round of people left. Kinda helps keep the community alive. Everyone always raves about my potatoes." He smiled proudly, and his tail wagged. "I'm sure Ellison'll be by in a few hours with the rest of what I need. He never disappoints."

Grant sat back, watching him curiously. "And after seven years, you don't think it's time to start paying for all these potatoes?"

"Pardon?"

"I know this place was really sheltered," Grant said. "And obviously, you couldn't be bringing stuff in and out without the queen's people knowing. But gold makes the world run, you know? And if you're not making any…"

PJ glanced at Pat nervously, sensing this conversation was getting a little too personal. But the dog-man didn't seem to have the capacity to be offended.

"I mean, we've got a lot of what we need here," Pat said after a moment. "Bill's a woodworker. Ingrid speaks to the trees to keep them from misbehaving. Hilde weaves baskets and other things. Inez—" He stopped, thinking. "No, Inez Pearlwind left, sorry. But she was our apothecary."

PJ snapped his fingers, recalling the names he'd learned back in Gilramore. "Inez Pearlwind? And her brother, too, right?"

Pat's smile widened. "You know them?"

"We ran into their sister in Gilramore a few weeks ago," PJ said, with a rush of happiness at connecting some dots. "They're all reunited and very happy, last I heard."

"Glad to hear that because she most decidedly was *not* when she left," Pat said with a sigh. "She and her brother hightailed it outta here before the sun set the day after we first heard the monster. A whole lotta folks who contributed to our village did, too." He let out a sniff. "I do hope you boys can figure out what's going on. It's gonna get lonely if everyone leaves. And Ellison's doing everything in his power to keep 'em here."

"Why?" PJ asked.

"'Cause he's a good man," Pat said, grinning.

PJ sat back, observing the dog-man for a moment. Was he just that loyal to Ellison? Or had he truly never considered the reasons behind Ellison's actions?

"What can you tell us about this monster?" Grant asked, leaning forward on the couch. "Surely you've been able to smell it?"

Pat eyed him curiously, and PJ almost smacked his friend for his bluntness. "What my associate is wondering is if you've seen the monster, or just heard it like everyone else?"

"Oh!" He nodded in understanding, his previous confusion evaporating like water on a hot day. "No. I tried to search the forest for any evidence, but whatever it is... I don't know. It's weird. It's not really leaving any trace of itself."

Could be someone pretending to be the monster. PJ

shook his head. He'd definitely seen something the day before.

"I don't go out into the forest too much if I can help it, you know? Ingrid's the only one who can do anything with it, and the rest of us know better than to tempt fate."

"What happens?" Grant asked, looking around the tree house nervously. "We heard a tree ate Melinda's reading chair."

Pat chuckled. "See, these trees are pretty old, and sometimes they forget that they let us live inside them. So they'll grow together overnight. Then Ingrid steps in and gets them to back off. Pretty cut and dried, though sometimes you've got to replace a few things. I'm sure Ellison'll make sure she has what she needs."

"It sounds like the trees are sentient," PJ said.

"Yeah." Pat didn't seem to find that alarming at all.

PJ decided to change the subject. "Did anyone here struggle with the forest restricting their magic?"

"Erm, in what way?" Pat tilted his head, much like a dog would when curious.

PJ considered him for a moment. Would a dog-headed man fear a dragon shifter? Or worse, would the confession of a lack of magic be to their detriment? He once again missed Tim's confident assessment of situations and found himself unable to come up with an answer.

"PJ's magical," Grant said after a long pause. "Doesn't seem to have full access to his powers here. Was that the case for anyone else powerful who lived here?"

"Not too many powerful folks to speak of," Pat said. "We had the Pearlwinds, of course, but they never had any sort of trouble. I'd probably put that question to Ellison. He's been around longer than any of us. Well, except Harold, I'd wager."

"You've met Harold?" PJ asked, confused. "Did he know about the enclave before the queen was overthrown?"

"No, he started showing up after we were free to come and go," Pat said. "But sorta wish he hadn't, you know? He's ornery and miserable."

"Yeah, what is *his* deal?" Grant asked.

"He hates magic," Pat said. "Ellison doesn't know it, but we all see it on his face when he delivers our supplies. Can barely stand to look at all of us, and surely lets us know we're trespassing, in his mind. He and Hilde got into it the other day." He snapped his fingers. "But you know, you should really talk to Ingrid."

"We hear she's busy," PJ said.

"Eh, she's not too busy to talk to you," Pat said, popping up. "C'mon, I'll take you there now."

CHAPTER FIVE

PJ still wasn't sure what to make of the forest controlling his magic, nor did he know what to make of the information he'd gotten about Ellison. He really was trying to keep things in perspective and not jump to conclusions, as he'd done in Padstow the week before. There, he'd accused the wealthy mine owner of sabotage, when she'd been trying to build a safety net for the town all along. Here, it seemed as though Ellison had been using his funds to help out of the goodness of his heart.

But Grant had made a point that it was a bit *too* generous. He'd foregone upkeep at his manor, save his garden, and that was only thanks to Harold not taking no for an answer. But everyone else *outside* the enclave had been sacked and had to make their own way. Did those folks know Ellison had been freely giving his gold to Forest Den? Was that part of the reason they detested him?

PJ wasn't going to volunteer that information to them, in any case. To be honest, he didn't even know if it was pertinent to the task at hand. Clearly, he'd seen a monster. Clearly, he'd just *heard* a monster.

He once again reached for Tim, frustrated when nothing came back.

"Do you think it could be a dragon?" Grant asked, as they fell in step behind Pat and passed three vacant tree houses with wood over the windows and empty planter boxes.

"Hm?"

"The roaring," Grant said. "Do you think it could be a dragon? Maybe we've inadvertently found someone actually in need of our dragon shifting services."

PJ considered the question, as the monstrous creature who'd eyed him the day before came back to the forefront of his mind. "If what we just heard is the same thing I saw yesterday, then no. Tim said it wasn't a dragon. When I could talk with him."

"Still nothing?" Grant asked.

"I'm sure he'll come out when we leave," PJ

said, not meeting his gaze. "Which I'd like to do. Tonight. If we can."

"If we leave, we won't get to see this monster in action," Grant pointed out.

PJ frowned. "Maybe we can sneak out for a second and come back, then."

As they passed a house with bright yellow and red flowers planted around the steppingstones, the orange door swung open and out walked a grumpy-looking woman with purple hair who barely came up to PJ's stomach. Bigger than a gnome, but not quite human, either. She didn't seem pleased to see Pat and definitely didn't look pleased to see the boys behind him.

"Who're these strangers?" she demanded. "And why are they here?"

"Oh, Ellison hired these boys—I think he hired you, didn't he?" Pat asked.

"In a manner of speaking," PJ said, before Grant could say anything.

"Well, they're here looking into all this racket," Pat continued. "Boys, this is Hilde. You haven't seen anything strange when you've been getting things for your baskets, right?"

The short woman eyed the boys. "No, but I was only a few steps out of the village yesterday. Could still see my house. Whatever's doing the ruckus-making is a ways out of the forest."

"What can you tell us about it?" PJ asked.

She put her hands on her hips. "Well, it happens in the middle of the night. Loudest thing I've ever heard. Comes with a bone-rattling thumping, too. Like something huge is approaching. But when we all come out, nothing but dark trees. Course, can't see anything in the middle of the night, so the thing could be standing just outside the village, and none of us would be the wiser."

"You can't feel it?" PJ asked.

"What?"

PJ swallowed, recalling the bone-deep fear when the monster had met his gaze. "I mean, erm… You're magical, right? So can you…feel it?"

"Nope." She didn't seem to think that was odd, either. "But I tell ya, Pat. If this thing keeps me up another night, I've got half a mind to pack up my house and head to my sister's."

"You can't *leave*," Pat said. "Oh, it's just a lot of noise, you know? Nothing to be worried about. Maybe just the forest being the forest."

"Yeah, the forest can be the forest," Hilde said with a grunt. "I like the peace and quiet here, but I don't like having to worry that my home's going to collapse in on itself or having a monster roaring all hours of the night. I'm not waiting around to be eaten or smooshed or whatever else this monster wants to do to us."

"Are you sure it wants to do something to you?" Grant asked. "It hasn't yet, has it?"

"Well, no..." She shifted. "No, all it's done is make a lot of noise. But it's only a matter of time, I'm sure."

"You really should reconsider, Hilde," Pat said. "These two boys will figure out what's going on."

"Hmph!" She scoffed. "They barely look old enough to hold their ale. Ellison's off his rocker, hiring them."

"We're more experienced than we look," Grant said. "We've solved a few problems in some other towns where people were in danger of losing homes and livelihoods."

"And what are you gonna do about it once you figure out what it is?" She folded her arms across her chest. "From the sounds of it, it could crush both of you with its pinkies."

"We'll cross that bridge when we come to it," Grant said. "Sometimes, the reason for the disruption isn't what it seems. Right, Peej?"

PJ nodded, not liking how everyone seemed to have the same idea of the monster—and how that matched what he'd seen.

"So what, are you here on behalf of the king?" Hilde said. "Ellison said he wrote to 'em for help. At least, that's what he told the Pearlwinds he was gonna do."

"Poor man's scrambling to do whatever it takes to keep us happy," Pat said with a sigh.

"Why?" Grant asked.

Hilde blinked at him. "What?"

"Why is he being so nice to you?" Grant asked. "Paying for your things, making deliveries. Asking for nothing in return when his own gold is running out." He shrugged. "Seems really kind, but…"

"He's a good man," Hilde said, her eyes flashing. "A great man. The best."

"He's wonderful, but even a good man's gold has to run out sometime," PJ said, though his own amulet had proven that to be untrue for the most part. "And he seems to have a few secrets he's not telling us."

"Because you two Nosy Nellies don't need to know," Hilde said. "Ellison's got more character, more backbone, more—"

"All right, all right," Pat said. "They didn't mean any harm. I'm sure they're just trying to sort everything out." He gestured to the boys. "C'mon, let's go find Ingrid, hm? See you tonight, Hilde!"

He hummed to himself as he plodded along the path, and PJ and Grant scrambled after him. He introduced a few more people who were poking their heads out from their homes to see who the strangers were but didn't come out like Hilde had.

PJ slowed his gait, letting Pat get farther ahead

of them. "Ellison's got a legion of loyal subjects."

"Mm. He's friendly with the king... Wait." Grant tilted his head toward Pat. "You think Pat's got dog hearing, too?"

PJ held his breath, waiting for Pat to turn around and confirm he was listening. But he kept walking, waving to people as they passed.

"We're safe, or he's going to pretend he's not listening," PJ said. "I'm getting the sense these folks will do whatever Ellison says."

"And Ellison might be out to pull the rug out from underneath them," Grant said. "Or someone's trying to pull the rug out from under Ellison. Harold, maybe. He looks mad enough to want to ruin his employer."

"Or any of the folks in the village." PJ shook his head. "But I *saw* a shadow, Grant. Something big and powerful and magical. Something that could be a typhon."

"I believe you," Grant said, almost thoughtfully. "But that doesn't mean it's the same thing we're dealing with in Forest Den, either."

PJ frowned, unsure what his friend was getting at, but their conversation stopped when Pat turned around to smile at them cheerfully.

"You two all right back there?" His tail wagged. "Not too much farther. This town used to be a tad bigger, but once the first wave of people left, a bunch of the trees picked up their roots and headed back into the forest."

PJ almost stumbled over his feet. "They… What?"

"Got up and left," Pat said, as if that were a normal thing trees did every day. "Oh, none of the homes that were inhabited, of course. Ingrid made sure of that. But the rest of 'em."

PJ and Grant shared a look of confusion but didn't press. The house they approached seemed to be missing one of the windows on the left side. In fact, the whole tree looked overgrown, almost, with large sections of the trunk bulging out.

Pat walked up to the door, which was halfway off its hinges, and knocked. "Melinda? Ingrid? Are you in here?"

"Yes!" came a soft, high voice from somewhere inside.

Pat squeezed his way through the door, and PJ made to follow.

Grant didn't budge. "That looks dangerous," he said with a frown. "And cramped."

"Fine," PJ said with a huff as he pushed his way around the overgrown tree trunk.

Inside, he found a homey cottage not unlike Pat's (save the dog fur), although there was a massive tree root growing off to the side. Beside it, a tall woman with dark brown skin, curly, puffy hair, and pointed ears stood with her hands over her mouth.

"All right, Melinda?" Pat asked.

"Does it look like I'm all right?" Melinda said with a sigh. "This tree, just…and overnight! I'm lucky my bed is on the other side, else I would've found myself encased in wood, too."

"Oh, you wouldn't be encased," said the soft voice from before. A lithe woman with olive green skin and dark green hair emerged from behind the tree root. She wore a crown of tree branches in her hair, and her clothes were flowy and ethereal as she swept her hands along the tree. "It would've pushed you from your bed, is all."

"It encased my bookshelf and reading chair," Melinda said with a scowl. "Can you fix it? It's okay if the shelf was eaten, but my books, Ingrid. My books."

"Just one moment." Like Pat, Ingrid gave off the impression that not much bothered her, least of all a large tree limb in the middle of the room. She inhaled deeply, closing her eyes and humming to herself. It was a soothing melody, and even PJ found his eyelids drooping as he fell into the rhythm of the notes. But he woke right up when the limb moved, groaning loudly as it pulled itself from the ground, slithering back into the outer tree. A bookshelf fell out, the contents spilling onto the floor with multiple *thumps*.

"Oh, goodness!" Melinda cried, running toward the books on the floor. "They're ruined, Ingrid! Half the pages are still missing."

Ingrid, who was still humming, though she'd moved to touch the outside of the room now that the big clump in the center was gone, opened one eye. "Could you release the rest of the pages, please?"

There was a loud cough that rumbled PJ's bones, and the ceiling spat out a stack of papers, which floated listlessly to the ground.

"Thanks," Melinda said dryly as she gathered them. "Oh, it's going to take ages to get this back together. How did this happen? I thought you were reminding the trees daily."

"I did, but this tree seems to be more forgetful than most," Ingrid said, a small furrow appearing in her brows as she patted the tree. "I can't say this won't happen again, and I'd hate for you to lose more of your precious books. I know how much they mean to you. It's probably best if we find you a new tree to live in."

Melinda sniffed as she looked through the pages, sorting them into piles. "Maybe it *is* time to leave. As much as Ellison doesn't want me to…"

"Why not?" PJ asked.

Melinda looked up, surprised. "Who're you?"

"Oh, sorry about that," Pat said. "This is PJ

Norris. He and his friend Grant have been hired by Ellison to look into the roaring. They said they wanted you to take them out into the forest, Ingrid, if you've got a chance."

Ingrid turned to PJ, surveying him closely. "Hm. The forest has been uneasy all morning. I thought it was because of the noise, but it's *you*, isn't it?"

"Me?" PJ swallowed, again worrying if his presence was making the problems worse. "I told it I didn't mean it any harm."

That familiar panic rose in his chest as he recalled Harold's words. How the typhon would be drawn to him.

But Ingrid's kind smile snapped him back to reality. "Telling and being are two different things, dear one. But..." She tilted her head, inhaling. "Hm. Interesting."

"What?"

"I've got a few more things to attend to before I'm free for the day, but you're welcome to come with me if you like." She turned to Melinda. "I hope you reconsider leaving. Ellison's promised he's got something important to share with us soon. And I know he wants you to be a part of it, the way you've been an indispensable part of our town since its inception."

"Between this monster in the woods and the

trees taking my property, I'm not sure it's worth it to stay," she said with a huff. Then, as if someone had cast a spell on her, she softened. "Then again, Ellison's been so kind. And he said he specifically wanted a crystal magic user around..."

"What's that?" Grant asked.

She nodded to an array of beautiful stones neatly arranged on her wall. "I use the power of stones to cast magic. Obviously, it didn't help with this tree." She gestured toward the house. "But for other things—intentions, small hurts, and improving a harvest—it works very well."

"Why would Ellison want a magic user like that around?" PJ asked, then when Melinda gave him a sideways look, he added, "I mean, obviously, it's quite helpful in a town like this. But..." He considered how to phrase it. "Couldn't he just call on you when he needed you if you left? Why is it important that you stay *in* the town?"

"I heard through the grapevine that he told the Pearlwinds—they were witches—that he wanted unique magical folks living here. For what purpose, I don't know. Maybe he just likes having a collection of us. Or maybe it has something to do with what his father did once upon a time. Either way..." She picked up another page. "As much as we all owe him for keeping us safe and fed, he can't control the forest. And if this monster keeps rattling our windows and keeping us up all night, we ought to just take the hint and leave."

THE HAMLET WITH THE MONSTER SITUATION

our windows and keeping us up all night, we ought to just take the hint and leave."

CHAPTER SIX

"So we have one town full of folks who hate Ellison," Grant muttered under his breath as they followed Ingrid. "And another full of people who have unwavering loyalty to him. What's he planning? And better question: do you think he'll tell us if we ask him outright?"

"I think if he wanted to tell us, he would've already," PJ said. "Erm, Ingrid? What are you doing?"

The green-skinned woman was practically floating from tree to tree, resting her hand on the bark for a moment before moving to the next. The trees seemed to shiver when she touched them, as if they'd been waiting for her to greet them all morning.

"Part of my daily ritual," she said, stopping at another tree. "I've got to wish each of these lovely creatures a good morning, remind them they're houses, and hear any concerns they might have." She paused at one of the vacant houses, tutting. "Really? Well, I'll have to have a word with Bill. Yes, I'm sure it's just a misunderstanding. We'll take care of it." She floated away, humming to herself as she reached out for the next tree.

"What did it say?" PJ asked.

"Apparently, Bill was taking a few too many liberties inside and caused some damage that the tree didn't like. He's such a reasonable fellow, and so I'll just have to remind him to take a bit more care. Some of these trees are more temperamental than others." She tapped a tree and laughed. "Not you, of course. You're a delight."

"So this is your magic?" PJ asked. "You can control the trees?"

"Control? Hardly." She giggled. "The forest was quite welcoming, of course, when we all needed refuge, but it can be ornery at times. So my job is to communicate with the trees and the inhabitants. Make sure everyone's getting along and solve any problems before the trees get too angry—and vice versa. "

"The forest doesn't like me very much," PJ said.

"I can tell," she said, nodding sagely. "You're constrained. There's power inside you, but you can't access it." She clicked her tongue, looking around at the nearby trees. "Cheeky forest. You're just a boy. What harm can you do?"

"I'm, er..." Heat rose in PJ's cheeks. "I'm a dragon shifter."

She turned to him, her mouth forming a small "o."' "As in a creature that breathes fire?"

He nodded.

"Right, well, I can see why the forest wouldn't want you free to do *that*," she said with a chuckle.

"My dragon has some other useful benefits," PJ said, thinking of how Tim could scan this entire forest and find the monster in moments. "Am I really the only magical creature the forest has contained?"

"There wasn't anyone who needed containment like you do," she said with a generous smile. "It's otherwise been a magnanimous host. When the first group of us arrived, scared for our lives, the trees made space for us. Hollowed out their interiors and welcomed us to add doors and windows, tickled at the chance to be home to more than just birds and other forest life." She sighed, lovingly stroking one of the long stems of a nearby plant. "But, as with any long-term relationships, disagreements can come up. Time passes and the trees forget, as you saw with Melinda. They're awfully apologetic, of course, but the damage is done. It's why I make sure to greet them most mornings. Just in case they start to lose their memories."

"Is that becoming more common?" PJ asked. "The trees forgetting?"

"No. Melinda's tree has done similar things before, though not quite as bad as today's incident. It's a very old and forgetful sort, which is why I recommended we move her to another house."

"The trees don't know anything about this monster, do they?" Grant asked.

She pursed her lips, thinking for a moment. "To be honest, I'm not sure what's going on. The forest is uneasy every night, and it's not telling me anything. Almost like someone's told it to keep quiet."

PJ frowned. "Someone else can talk to the trees like you can?"

"No one that I'm aware of," she said. "And it's hard to translate tree-talk sometimes, especially when they all have something to say. Each individual tree has its own thoughts and ideas, you know. And they can pick and choose if they want to talk with me. Some of the trees farther out aren't very chatty, so I let them be. It's the same as with any group of people, you know. Everyone may want to work toward the same goal, but we all have minds of our own. So it is with trees."

"Surely, the ones closer in have given you something," PJ said.

She shook her head. "This forest is very large and very old. It contains a lot of secrets—ones that were too deep for the queen's people to reach. If there was such a creature, I wouldn't put it past the forest to hide its identity from me."

"Do you think the forest wants you guys to leave?" Grant asked.

"I don't think so," she said, after considering the question. "At least, not in those terms. And trees have a way of being quite blunt when they have a mind to be."

She leaned in and touched another trunk. "Well, that's awfully kind of you. Thank you." She removed her hand and turned back to the boys. "This tree would love to have Melinda move in. It really does miss its former owners."

"Pat said a lot of folks left the first night you heard the monster," PJ said.

"Monster is sometimes in the eye of the beholder," she said with a sigh. "I think some of them were looking for an excuse. As grateful as we all are to Ellison, and to this forest, it's not a place where one makes their living easily." She sighed.

"Yeah, but it seems like Ellison's trying to do

something to that end, isn't he?" Grant asked. "Bill's building furniture for him, isn't he? Where does Bill source the wood?"

"The forest allows him an allotment of branches and the like, and I think he gets some extra planks delivered by Ellison."

"You said that Bill was being too careless with one tree, though," PJ said.

"Yes, that particular tree was complaining that he'd been too hard with the hammer and nails when he was installing a small cabinet near the kitchen in one of the vacant houses. Which is odd for Bill, because he's always been so careful." She sang to herself as she continued, but the boys stayed back a few steps.

"Who's Bill building the furniture for?" PJ asked.

"Some of the recently vacated houses," she said. "Ellison's asked me to ensure the trees keep them as houses, so I do. Says they will be inhabited shortly."

"Who's going to live in them?" Grant asked.

She shrugged. "I'm sure I'll be enlightened eventually." She turned to them with a kind smile. "Well, I'm finished with my morning chores. Would you two like to start your trek into the forest?"

"Y-yeah," PJ said, though he really wasn't looking forward to it. Here in the clearing, talking with the townsfolk who'd lived here for years, the nervous energy of the surrounding forest was held at bay. But if he were to step inside, it would certainly come back with a vengeance.

Grant, of course, had no issues following Ingrid into the forest, but PJ lingered on the edge for a moment, wishing for the umpteenth time he could reach his dragon. But even as he did, a trickle of shame flitted across his mind. Tim had already harangued him for his fearful dreams, and surely, the dragon would have *a lot* to say about PJ's dithering.

You dragon, he'd said.

"Just one problem with that right now," PJ said, casting his gaze around. "I'm not really a dragon. I'm just PJ, without any magic to speak of."

But the forest before him was stitching itself closed, and if he didn't unstick his feet from the ground, he'd be left in the village. Not the best look for a magical investigator.

So with a hard swallow, he strode forward, just as the path disappeared behind him.

~

You dragon. You dragon. You dragon.

PJ kept this refrain in his mind as he trailed behind Grant and Ingrid through the thick underbrush. He'd been tripping over his feet and struggling to walk on the way in, but now the forest was even wilder and the terrain more difficult to navigate. Ingrid didn't seem to have any problems, lithely moving between the trees and bushes, avoiding the low branches and thorns with an ease that Grant and PJ could never aspire to. But as PJ finally caught up with her, he realized that the *forest* was sparing her these injuries—physically moving itself to avoid touching her.

"Okay, so now we've got Bill furnishing the vacant houses, and Ellison telling the trees they're going to be inhabited soon," Grant whispered. "What do you make of that whole conversation? 'Monster is in the eye of the beholder.' Do you think she knows something she's not sharing? Maybe she's in on it with Ellison?"

PJ kept his gaze on the ground to avoid tripping. "She wouldn't be helping us if she was in on it."

"Is she helping us, or keeping us from finding the truth?" Grant wagged his eyebrows. "She could be acting all flighty but really hiding a devilish secret. Maybe she's working with the forest, and they *both* want everyone else to leave?"

PJ shook his head. "I'm not getting that sense from her."

"So maybe," Grant said, catching himself on a small sapling so he didn't trip over an exposed root, "maybe we should focus on who knows about Ellison's plans? Maybe someone in the village—

Hilde, perhaps?—knows he's doing something, and they don't want him to do it."

"Why Hilde?"

"She mentioned she liked how peaceful and quiet it was," Grant said. "If Ellison's selling the tree houses to new people, then it might not be so quiet. Maybe she wants to put a stop to it."

"Maybe…" Hilde had also been quite affronted when they'd besmirched Ellison's character.

"Either way, our best bet is to find out who knows about Ellison's plans, whatever they are," Grant finished.

"Or," PJ said, glancing at the trees above, "there's a monster lurking around the village."

"Okay, whoever our culprit is put the monster up to it, then," Grant said. At PJ's dubious look, he shrugged. "Stranger things have happened, my friend. Wouldn't be surprised if it's some whole conspiracy."

"I think the last two towns have made you paranoid. Have a little faith in people. Maybe they'll surprise you in a good way."

"Or, maybe it's the old farmer trying to frame the kids, like in Padstow."

"That's not what it ended up being in Padstow."

"Close enough," Grant said. "I don't trust any of 'em. They all got secrets—even Ingrid."

"I think we're dealing with something real this

time," PJ said. "Because, as I'll remind you, I definitely saw something yesterday. And with what Harold said—"

"Harold was trying to scare you," Grant said. "Which is ridiculous. Need I remind you, you're a —"

"Regular person without access to my dragon," PJ snapped. Grant was starting to sound like Tim. "And who knows if Harold was trying to scare me or was actually telling the truth? If you felt what I did yesterday..." He shivered. "I've never sensed anything like that before."

"Peej." Grant eyed him. "Don't get wound up again."

"I'm not," he said, shifting. "I'm just trying to look at the angles."

"The angles are that we've got a formerly rich guy who's made an enemy of everyone in the small town just outside his door," Grant said. "Plus, we have a town full of magical creatures said formerly rich guy is trying to keep around for some mysterious reason. Magical creatures he used all his gold on for another mysterious reason." He gestured toward the trees. "And a sentient forest that kinda looks like it might be tired of housing said magical creatures. I really don't think a monster is in this at all."

PJ just made a noise instead of arguing. "As

soon as we finish this loop through the forest, I want to get out of here. Get some insight from Tim."

"You lived a long time without him," Grant said. "Are you really so reliant on him after just two weeks?"

Warmth crept up PJ's neck again. "It's not that I'm reliant, it's that… He has a way of framing things. It's good to have a second opinion."

"And mine doesn't count for anything?" Grant asked.

"You don't know magic like Tim does," PJ said. "I absolutely trust your opinion and judgment, but…"

"I get it, I get it." Grant pursed his lips. "But what I do know is what we've been through. First town, we thought it was the witch, but it was really some random fairy because we failed to see that everyone who was attacked had been chopping down wood. Second town, we thought it was the rich gal trying to sabotage the town, turned out it was the farmer doing something selfish." He ticked off his fingers. "There's a good chance someone's doing something underhanded. That's all I'm saying."

"But I saw—"

"And what if someone—say, that Harold fellow —is trying to make you *think* the typhon's making all this noise?" Grant said. "In order to scare you off?

Maybe he's tired of Ellison playing around in the forest, and he set up this whole charade to get everyone to leave? Pat said he thought everyone was trespassing. Maybe he's our culprit."

"How could he be?" PJ asked pointedly. "Seriously. How would a gardener make a noise like a monster? How would he be able to instill the power I felt when, I'll remind you, Tim was right there?"

"Well, that's what we're going to find out," Grant said with a wink before raising his voice to call to their forest guide, "Say, Ingrid, what do you know about Harold?"

"We don't cross paths much," she said mildly. "He works for Ellison, and he brings the rest of the town what they need to live comfortably. I can tell he loves plants. I've caught him staring at my garden when he comes and goes. That's probably why the forest let him in when it didn't allow the others."

"Others?" Grant asked. "You mean the folks from Cheshireville?"

"They were not coming in a spirit of good faith," she said simply. "So the forest did what the forest does and protected the inhabitants."

"You said Ellison's asked you to tell the vacant trees not to leave," Grant said. "That means he's expecting new people to come to town, right?"

"Suppose it does," she said lightly as she climbed

up a nearby hill with relative ease.

"Then," Grant huffed, as the hill seemed to shift to a higher incline, "will the forest let them in?"

"If their intentions are..." She stopped. "Oh. This is new."

PJ and Grant hurried up the rest of the hill, peering over the crest to the small clearing below.

There, in the center, was a gigantic human-shaped footprint.

CHAPTER SEVEN

"That's...um..." Grant stammered.

"Do you believe me now?" PJ asked with a quirked brow. On the one hand, the vindication was sweet. But on the other, that did mean they would eventually have to contend with the gigantic monster he'd seen in the forest. There were five toes and a human-shaped sole, but it was so immense it was hard to imagine the size of the thing that had made it—even though PJ had *definitely* seen it.

Grant, as usual, would rather stick a needle in his eye than be wrong. "Okay, it's a footprint. Doesn't mean that's what we're looking for. Could be coincidental, you know?"

"Why don't we see what the trees have to say?"

Ingrid said lightly.

The trio crept down the side of the clearing, PJ's gaze darting between the underbrush and the forest around them. How long ago had this footprint been made? Was the creature nearby? PJ could see pretty far, and although his logical mind said he would probably see the being that made a footprint longer than he was tall, his nerves were quite sure it was lurking just above him.

If only Tim were around, he thought mournfully.

"Hm." Ingrid attempted to place her hand on one of the thin saplings, but, to PJ's astonishment, the entire tree pulled itself out of the ground and moved away from her, almost petulantly swaying its branches as it faded into the rest of the trees.

"Was that one of the temperamental trees you were talking about?" PJ asked Ingrid.

She nodded. "Let me try another one."

But the entire space was filled with trees that didn't want to talk, which caused even unflappable Ingrid to furrow her brow.

"Well, that's definitely new," she said, after a moment. "Typically, even when there's a cluster that's not quite as chatty to the magical folks, there are at least one or two who'll give me a few moments of their time. But to have the entire lot be so angry?" She shook her head. "Strange."

"You know what else is strange?" Grant said,

turning around in the center of the footprint. "There's no path."

"What do you mean?" PJ asked.

"Well, okay, you saw a creature that was as tall as the trees," Grant said. "This footprint matches that, okay. But…" He gestured toward either end of the footprint. "A creature that size shoulda also made a path through the trees, right?"

"Unless they moved out of the way for him," PJ said. "The way they've done for Ingrid."

Grant pursed his lips. "Fine. Let's find another footprint, then."

The trio headed in the direction the footprint suggested, with Grant leading the way, Ingrid in the middle, and PJ holding up the rear. Every so often, Ingrid would ask a nearby tree a question and would nod at the answer, revealing nothing. It was hard to tell the location of the sun through the canopy, but as soon as the light took on an orange hue, and they'd found no more footprints, PJ called a halt to the expedition.

"We should turn back before it gets too dark to see," he said. "I don't think we're going to find another footprint."

"Agreed," Ingrid said. "None of the trees I've spoken to have seen a large creature. I don't think it came this way."

Grant scowled. "Couldn't you have said that

earlier?"

She shrugged. "I was waiting for the two of you to stop."

"Can you lead us back to the village, then?" PJ asked. "I'm not sure I know where we are."

"But of course." She nodded with that same ethereal smile. "Though we can take a different route back and perhaps ask more trees if they've seen anything they want to share."

The walk back to the village was the same as the one leaving it; lots of trees, a few who didn't want to talk with Ingrid, and nothing else to speak of. PJ kept glancing at the sky, nerves blossoming in his chest. What if they got lost in the woods overnight without his dragon to keep an eye out for monstrous creatures?

"You okay?" Grant asked under his breath. "Sense something?"

"No, and that's the problem," PJ said. "What are we gonna do if Ingrid can't get us back?"

"She's going to get us back," he said, giving PJ a sideways look. "You're jumpy. It's not like you."

"I don't want to run into this monster, that's all," PJ said. "I mean, you saw the size of the footprint. Something like that could snap us both in two if it had a mind to."

"I saw something that looked like a big footprint," Grant said with a look around. "I'm not sure that's what it was, though. Especially because there was no other evidence. No broken trees, no crushed plants, no clear way a creature that size came or went. Just a single, solitary footprint."

PJ blinked at him. "What are you trying to say?"

"I think someone dug a bunch of holes in the ground to make us think it's a footprint," Grant said.

"It was exactly the size of the creature I saw," PJ snapped, irritation climbing up his spine.

Grant shrugged.

PJ scowled. "Well, when we get out of here, I'll ask Tim, and I'm sure he'll be in agreement with me."

"Will he?"

PJ turned away, annoyed. To be sure, he'd been concerned about the harangue Tim would give him once free to speak again. *You dragon* had been in his mind. But on the other hand, the evidence was clear —a footprint matching the shadow.

Then again, Grant had painted a logical picture of Harold, intent on scaring everyone, planting the idea of the typhon in PJ's mind then placing all kinds of evidence to reinforce that notion. Harold, who hated strangers and the magical folks in Forest Den, would definitely hate the idea of Ellison allowing more people in.

Yet, PJ had been *sure*—positive, in fact—that

he'd seen that typhon.

He tried once more for his dragon, pushing against the magic keeping them apart. The echo of Tim's presence sounded from somewhere in the distance, but it was still too far to reach.

He slowed, letting Grant and Ingrid fall a little way ahead of him then pulled his amulet out from under his shirt. He'd worn his old amulet continuously since the grannies had first given it to him. In fact, the only time he'd removed it was to replace it with his new one—and to communicate with the grannies.

But now, with this forest keeping him from Tim, would it be so bad if he removed his amulet while still inside? Would it allow him to have access to his dragon finally?

"What are you doing?" Grant asked, watching him suspiciously.

"Nothing," PJ said, stuffing the amulet back in his shirt. "Just thinking."

By the time they spotted Forest Den, it was the *only* thing visible through the trees. A thick mist had descended on the forest as the sun had set, casting everything in muted tones. And while PJ was quite sure the sun and moon still existed above the canopy, they weren't providing any sort of light to walk by.

"It's going to be fun getting back to Cheshireville," Grant said with a grunt as he tripped over another root. "You think Ellison made it back?"

"Oh, you boys shouldn't even attempt that," Ingrid said, carefully avoiding a thorny bush. "The forest is dangerous enough during the daylight hours, but even more so at night. Even I avoid leaving if I can help it."

A jolt of fear shot through PJ. He'd wanted to talk to Tim tonight. Was he going to have to wait until sunup? What if the typhon showed up to grind his bones?

"But dinner?" Grant continued, looking at PJ for help. "And where are we to sleep?"

"Don't you worry about that," Ingrid said. "You're more than welcome to come to our communal dinner."

"Oh, right, Pat mentioned you guys do that," Grant said, visibly relaxing.

"When the town was fuller, one of the kitchen witches set up a de facto tavern. You probably noticed it earlier—lots of mushrooms situated near one of the trees."

PJ nodded.

"Well, Ephraim left, and so did the tavern, but the tables and chairs remained. Since we'd gotten so few in number, we started gathering just after sundown to connect, then folks started bringing dinner, and now it's a daily ritual for all of us. I'll be bringing my teas, but there will be stews and bread and all manner of delicious things. I'll be sure to spread the word that there are two extra mouths to feed tonight."

"That's very kind of you," PJ said.

"But where are we going to *sleep?*" Grant moaned.

"Some of the vacant houses have beds," Ingrid said with a little chuckle. "Let's check with Bill to see which one he's finished with. I don't want to get in the middle of his work, but I have to assume there are a few ready for habitation."

She floated toward one of the tree houses, and Grant looked somewhat satisfied. "Well, at least we'll probably get a good look at that monster."

PJ shivered. "Let's hope it takes a night off."

"Let's hope otherwise," Grant said, nudging him. "How are we gonna catch Harold red-handed if there's nothing to catch?"

PJ bit his tongue instead of arguing. Grant would see—when that monster showed up, it wouldn't be fun and games. Even as PJ followed Ingrid toward one of the vacant houses, foreboding crawled up his chest.

Ingrid rapped on one of the non-decorated houses and opened the door. "Bill?"

Inside, the house looked to be under

construction. The centaur was measuring long planks of wood propped between two sawhorses. Nearby sat what would be a circular table that was in mid-construction with only half the planks installed. There were freshly painted cabinets hanging from the small kitchen area and a rocking chair in front of a magical fireplace, which held a blue flame that seemed to emit cold instead of heat.

"Ingrid," Bill said. "Did you find something?"

"A footprint," PJ said.

"*Kind of* a footprint," Grant corrected. "We're not sure what we found, to be honest."

"The fact of the matter is we spent a bit too much time in the forest," Ingrid said. "Now it's too dark to leave. I was hoping they could stay the night at one of the houses you've been fixing up for Mr. Thornhill." She glanced around the unfinished quarters. "Not this one, obviously. But I think the Pearlwinds left a pair of beds in their house, didn't they?"

Bill nodded slowly. "They did. But I'm not sure Mr. Thornhill—"

"He won't mind," she said with a wave of her hand. "I'm sure he was hoping they'd sleep here tonight, so they can see the monster for themselves."

"We're not hoping for it to appear tonight," Bill said, glancing at the boys. "As good as it would be for you two to see it, it's not a fun experience. And I fear it might set Hilde on her way for good."

"Either way," Ingrid said, a little impatiently, "these two dears need a place to rest their heads. I'm sure you can help them, can't you?" She flashed him a smile. "I did manage to smooth things over with Killwin's former tree house earlier. It was right put out with you for being too hard on the hammering. It was ready to close in on itself and leave just this morning."

Bill let out a breath, clearly understanding what she was getting at. "Fine. But if Mr. Thornhill has anything to say about it, I'm sending him to you."

~

Bill led PJ and Grant to a cozy little tree house off the beaten path. PJ sensed a familiar thread of latent witch magic as he walked up to the tree, much like perfume lingering in a room after someone had left. It made him smile, reminding him of the Pearlwinds and that this world wasn't quite as big as he'd thought. The witches from Gilramore *and* the ogres from Padstow had both lived in this enclave. Who might he meet in the future from Forest Den? It was a nice thought exercise, and one that effectively distracted him from thinking about the night ahead—and what might come out of the dark forest.

"Any reason Ellison wouldn't want us to stay in a vacant house?" Grant asked as Bill walked up to the door and pulled out a large ring of keys. "And why is he in charge of who stays here anyway? Does he own these properties?"

"It's a bit of a gray area, to be sure," Bill said, sifting through the keys. "In my mind, he as good as paid for the village with all he provided over the years. And still provides."

"So he's planning on selling them," Grant said with a nod.

Bill eyed him. "His plan isn't mine to share. You'll have to ask him."

"Did he come back?" PJ asked, looking around. "He said he was going to deliver more potatoes."

"He came and went already."

The centaur was so tall he had to duck as he walked inside, and his hooves made a loud clopping noise as he padded across the living room. PJ's eyes adjusted to the darkness, and he immediately caught the scent of fresh-cut wood. There was a new dining room set in the corner but also set of rocking chairs near an unlit hearth, and a pair of beds near the back of the room.

"It's lovely," PJ said. "But why the new furniture? If he's selling it."

"Mr. Thornill's request," he said, simply. "And he's not planning to sell anything. At least, not that he's told me."

Based on his curtness, it was probably wise to

change the subject, lest they find themselves sleeping outside. Instead, PJ turned to inspect one of the nearby chairs, admiring the artistry. "It's beautiful work."

"Thank you," Bill said, running his hand along the table in the small kitchen space. "I just got this place put together this morning. But I've got ten more on my list I need to get done before..." His tail swished. "Well, Mr. Thornhill isn't really ready to share all that yet."

"Hm." PJ walked into the kitchen and opened the recently constructed cabinets, finding them bare. Good thing there was that potluck later. "Thank you for the hospitality, Bill. We appreciate it. The day clearly got away from us."

"One...favor," Bill said. "I know there's bound to be conversation about what you've seen in the forest. I'm not sure what that might be, but if you could keep your comments to yourselves, or at least try, to keep the townsfolk from panicking..." He sighed. "There are already enough nerves to go around without you adding to them."

"You want us to lie to them?" PJ said.

"To be fair, we didn't find much," Grant said. "A footprint that might not be a footprint."

"It was a footprint," PJ said.

"Just be careful how you phrase things," Bill said. "That's all I'm asking. We'll be gathering to eat in about an hour or so. But if you need anything else, don't hesitate to ask." He pointed to a tree twenty feet away. "My house is right over there."

"Well, this is fine." As soon as the door closed, Grant flopped down onto the nearest mattress. "At least it's a bed. Pretty coincidental the Pearlwinds lived here. Small world, eh?"

"Yeah." PJ lingered by the window, gazing out at the forest beyond. He was uneasy about staying here, not only because it delayed his necessary chat with Tim, but also because…well, would he draw the monster into the village?

Grant says there isn't a monster, came the calm, rational part of his brain.

The footprint. The shadow. The roaring. Something is out there. And it wants to—

"I'm going to walk around," PJ said, if only to quiet the voices in his mind. He didn't wait for Grant to respond, hurrying out the door, even though the air seemed just as fresh inside the cabin as outside. The magical pressure weighed heavily on him, too, and he had half a mind to keep walking until he saw the stars again. The forest didn't like him; perhaps it would let him leave?

"Remember what Ingrid said," PJ muttered to himself. "Dangerous forest."

"You talkin' to yourself?"

PJ stopped, realizing Hilde was watching him. "Sorry?"

"You're muttering to yourself like a mad person," she said. "Are you well?"

"Very," PJ said with a nervous smile. "Erm. See you at dinner?"

Ignoring her scrutiny, he scurried away, his hands stuffed in his pockets. But unfortunately, he couldn't go too far before he was hit with the wall of trees (and the palpable magic) that kept him trapped in the village.

"I'm not trapped," he muttered to himself, glancing up. "Just momentarily detained. For my own safety. Not as if I want to be wandering around in the dark, to be stepped on…"

He walked the perimeter, his sense of direction warped by all the similarities around him and lack of light. Night had all but fallen, and the darkness beyond had come alive with cricket chirps and leaves rustling. It would've been soothing if not for his already frayed nerves.

"Could you please let me have a little access to my dragon?" PJ asked the misty woods beyond.

Something invisible pushed against him, which PJ took for a no.

He stopped at a fallen tree and plopped down on it, staring into the darkness with a frown. His amulet weighed on his neck, so he yanked it out, inspecting the inscriptions and markings. Then, with a breath, he pulled it off and waited for it to glow.

Nothing happened.

"Can you find the grannies?"

The faintest of glows emitted from the golden rim, but that was it.

"Drat."

He placed the amulet on the ground, casting another look at it to make sure no one was watching him, then took a step back. His plan, as silly as it was, was to test the distance. If he got far enough away from the amulet, its dampening effect might ease up enough that Tim could come out.

He crept farther away, inch by inch, waiting for the pressure in his chest to ease or Tim's clear voice to ring out.

Then, to his horror, a black shadow darted from the forest and snatched up the amulet, before disappearing into the forest.

"No!"

All previous trepidation forgotten, PJ dashed into the darkness after the creature, thinking for a split second how lucky he was that the forest *let him pass*. But that gratitude was quickly forgotten as he followed the glint from the amulet bobbing along in the distance, as if being carried by something struggling to keep it aloft. It drifted higher, then sank like a stone, then rose back up again. PJ's heart pounded in his chest as he pushed through the forest, ignoring the way the branches smacked into his face. The only thing that mattered was getting that amulet back.

Finally, the glint stopped moving, settling about five feet above PJ's head. It was hard to make out exactly what he was looking at, until a beak clapped and a loud *caw caw* shook him to his bones.

"That's mine," PJ said, hoping he sounded more confident than he felt. "Give it back."

The bird hopped around on the branch it was sitting on, the amulet dangling above PJ's head. It didn't seem sentient (or at least, not to the point where it could hold a conversation), and PJ got the distinct impression it had stolen his amulet because it was shiny, not because it knew what it did.

"Fine," PJ huffed. "I guess I'll have to come get it."

He walked to the tree, running his hands along the bark. Then, recalling the way Ingrid had said every tree in the forest had a mind of its own, he retreated.

"Hi, erm…tree. I'm PJ. That bird's stolen my amulet. And if I don't get it back, once I leave the forest, I could turn into a nasty dragon who could burn everything down."

He paused, thinking that might cause the forest to *never* let him leave.

"I don't want to do that, so if you'd be so kind as to let me climb you so I can retrieve my amulet, that would be nice. I—"

The tree shivered under his fingertips, and he jumped back, bracing himself for whatever the tree was going to do to him. The bird above flew off, cawing angrily to the night, and, after a few more shakes, the amulet broke loose, falling right into PJ's hands.

He quickly slid it around his neck with relief. "Thank you."

The tree shivered.

"Look…" PJ considered his words. "I'm not sure why the forest doesn't trust me, but I'm really not here to cause problems. Ellison—he lives just beyond the forest, I think you probably know him

—he's worried about the people in here. And yeah, I know you did a great job of protecting them from the queen, but whatever is roaming around, if you could tell it to just roam somewhere else so folks could sleep at night, that would be great."

Even in the darkness, the forest was teeming with activity, and he could almost hear the forest talking back to him.

"And if it's really you trying to expel the people to get back to what you were before the people arrived, then please inform Ingrid so she can tell the rest of the town," PJ said.

Again, that invisible force pushed at him.

"No?" PJ frowned. "That's not what's going on?"

A path opened in front of him—even the canopy pulled back to reveal the moonlight. Despite his reservations, PJ followed it, holding his breath and girding himself for what he might find. The forest was leading him toward a rock in the middle of a clearing.

No, not a rock, he realized. Something covered with a dark blanket.

"Odd," PJ muttered, kneeling.

He pulled back the sheet to reveal…a collection of vases. He picked one up, turning it around and running his fingers along the edge. He opened the top and sniffed, sensing nothing but earthen clay.

The others were the same. Empty pots with nothing inside.

"If you're trying to show me something, I'm not getting it, but I'll keep it in mind," PJ said. "Do you think you could get me back to Forest Den?"

The forest cleared a path once more, and PJ left the vases, replaced the blanket, and followed. He could've asked to go back to the village beyond, but Grant would worry if he disappeared, and… somehow, he was feeling a bit more confident about his abilities. He hadn't needed Tim to converse with the forest, and it had trusted him enough to show him, well, something it wanted him to know. It, at least, wasn't trying to evict the citizens of Forest Den. One less suspect on his list.

Boom. Boom. Boom.

PJ stopped in his tracks, a chill running down his spine. Something *big* was nearby. The ground shuddered with every step, and PJ held his breath, waiting for the thing to emerge. He scanned the canopy, the space between the trees, spinning in place as he searched for the source of the danger.

Nothing.

"Forest?" PJ muttered. "What am I looking at?"

In the distance, at the end of the path he was walking, the trees parted, and a pale head at the same level as the tallest limbs of the trees glinted in the moonlight. PJ's heart dropped to his stomach, especially as the thing seemed to notice the small dragon shifter at the end of the path. He didn't have red eyes, like in PJ's dreams, but PJ sensed his attention the same way he'd sensed it the day before. It was all-encompassing. Unmistakable. Terrifying.

Had the forest led him here to be squashed?

"T-Tim, now would be a g-good t-time to come out," PJ said, backing up.

But, of course, the dragon was nowhere to be found.

He waited, his entire body on pins and needles, for what would happen next.

To his surprise, the gigantic creature turned away from him and kept walking.

PJ was afraid to breathe. What had just happened?

The forest closed the path ahead of him, the one leading toward the giant (the typhon?), and opened another that cut hard to the left. Still shaking, PJ had no other choice but to follow it, wondering what in the world the forest was doing—and why he'd been spared twice now if this monster was so invested in removing the people of Forest Den.

~

Fortunately, the new path led him right back to the magical enclave. PJ had never been happier to see anything in his life. He made a beeline for the house he and Grant were staying in but found it empty. Light conversations reached his ears, and he scanned the small village, finally spotting the townsfolk around the collection of mushrooms that had once been the tavern.

Remembering what Bill had said about worrying the townsfolk, he tried to shake off his nerves. He didn't think it prudent to mention he'd seen the typhon, especially since…well, nothing had come of it. The typhon could've walked right toward PJ, scooped him up, and crushed him before he'd had a second thought, but he didn't.

"Where've you been?" Grant snapped, spotting PJ immediately. From the concern etched on his face, Grant had actually been worried about him.

Ingrid, too, approached with a furrow between her brows. "You went out in the forest, didn't you?"

"I, erm…" PJ cleared his throat. "A thief snatched something of mine. I went to get it back. Took me a little while, but the forest returned me here. Looks like it's not quite as mad at me as we thought."

"Does that mean we can head back to the inn?" Grant asked. Unsaid was the reason: *So you can talk to Tim again?*

"I don't think so. It very clearly led me back here," PJ said, hoping his friend would get the hint and not pry. "But we'll talk about that later. I'm famished. What's for dinner?"

"Come on," Ingrid said, gently taking his arm. "It's a nice spread tonight."

She led PJ to one of the larger mushrooms being used as a table. Waiting in a hodgepodge of pots and pans were roasted vegetables, meat stew, what appeared to be a casserole with green and brown beans, mashed potatoes, gravy, and even an apple crisp. Off to the side was a large bowl of salad greens with ripe tomatoes and pungent purple onions, along with a basket of crusty bread.

Ingrid pressed a plate into PJ's hands with a smile. "Take as much as you like. We've all had a plate, but we were waiting on you to return to get seconds."

"I'm sorry," PJ said. "I guess I didn't realize the time."

"Not to worry." She squeezed his arm before releasing it. "Just glad the forest was kind enough to send you back here. I'd hate to think of you spending the evening at the mercy of whatever else lives beyond this place."

PJ wanted to tell her he'd seen the typhon, but Bill was standing close enough that he could overhear, and the centaur was eyeing PJ curiously. Instead, PJ took his overly full plate and sat next to Grant on one of the toadstools. It was surprisingly soft, yet held his weight well, and he tucked in, taking in the scene around him.

He counted no more than fifteen people, most of whom he'd seen earlier in the day. He was introduced to Delaney and Audra, a pair of nymphs with blue hair and skin, who managed the water wellspring for the rest of the village, and a human-sized creature named Senda who closely resembled an ogre, with green muscles and large horns, and who knitted and made the quilts PJ and Grant would be sleeping under tonight. They met more townsfolk who provided services and others with unique kinds of magic. Despite their different abilities, they smiled at each other with an ease and familiarity that told PJ this was a close community. But he couldn't help but notice the furtive glances toward the forest, and the way they seemed a hair on edge, like they were waiting for something to happen.

"So?" Hilde prompted, sitting atop a larger toadstool. "Did you boys find whatever's lurking in the woods?"

Bill eyed PJ and Grant, a hint of warning in his gaze.

"We're still gathering evidence," Grant said, as PJ couldn't lie as easily. "But if you ask me, it's clear someone's going through a lot of trouble to make it *look* like something scary."

"Why would they do that?" Audra asked.

"That's the question, isn't it?" Grant replied

with a look at Bill.

A blush appeared on Bill's bare chest and crept up toward his pale cheeks. "I'm not sure why you're looking at me."

"Well, you're doing a bunch of stuff for Mr. Thornhill," Hilde said, sniffing. "And he won't tell us what he's planning, only that he's planning it and it'll be worth our while to stick around."

Grant winked and pointed at her. "Exactly."

"I don't see what Mr. Thornhill's plans have to do with this monster lurking beyond our borders," Bill said.

"Because, as I said, I'm pretty sure there isn't a monster," Grant replied. "There's just a rumor, and someone's taking advantage of that. Someone who wants all you fine folks to vacate the town, either to disrupt Ellison's plans or because of some other reason we've yet to uncover."

"There's no monster at all?" Delaney said, looking at her wife. "Someone's making the earth move and creating that roaring sound?"

PJ swallowed, recalling the way he'd nearly lost his footing when the typhon walked by.

"I mean, with magic, anything's possible, isn't it?" Grant said, blissfully ignorant of PJ's concerns.

The townsfolk shared a nervous look, as if they weren't quite ready to believe that.

"Ingrid," Pat said, chewing on a raw cut of meat.

"You're the forest whisperer. What do you say?"

The dryad, who was the only one eating the salad, put down her fork. "As I told the boys earlier, the forest hasn't been forthcoming about the strange occurrences. It tells me what it wants me to know, and nothing more." She sat back. "Shall we tell them about the footprint?"

"Footprint?" Hilde sat up as Bill scowled at her. "What kind of footprint?"

"One that would fit the size of the creature we're supposedly looking for," Ingrid said.

"I don't think we need to worry ourselves unnecessarily," Bill said, cutting her off with a bit of a harsh tone. "I, for one, think it might be the most plausible that someone's just trying to cause us trouble, as these boys have said."

"Then why don't you tell us what Mr. Thornhill is doing?" Hilde said.

"You can ask him yourself," Bill replied hotly. "He'll be back in the morning. But in the meantime, we should keep our heads on straight. So far, all we've heard is a bunch of noise. No one's been hurt. No one's even *seen* anything." He nodded to Grant. "I'm more apt to believe this kid's right."

Grant's chest puffed with the encouragement. "I know it probably seems scary. But we've been around these sorts of investigations a few months now—"

"A couple of weeks," PJ muttered under his breath.

"And it's always something you don't expect," Grant continued. "It's *never* an actual monster. So in light of that, if anyone has anything they'd like to share, Peej and I are all ears."

ROOOOOAR.

CHAPTER NINE

PJ's heart sank into his stomach as he jumped to his feet. The sound was unlike anything he'd ever heard before, though it didn't seem to reverberate through him the way seeing the monster had. The roaring echoed through the village, followed by an ominous *thump, thump, thump* that made the tankards rattle and the stew ripple in the villagers' bowls.

"Run!" Audra cried, grabbing her wife's hand and making a mad dash away from the dining room.

The rest of the townsfolk didn't need to be told twice, leaving their half-eaten food on the table and bounding back to their homes as fast as they could walk or fly. Even Pat, who'd seemed unbothered by anything, let out a dog-like yelp as he ran on all fours back to his tree house. And Ingrid, too, headed quickly to her home, though she looked more perplexed than fearful, her green eyes sweeping the canopy with a furrow between her brow before disappearing behind her door.

Grant scrambled to his feet, running at full speed back to the house, with Bill right behind him. They both slammed their doors shut in unison, after which PJ realized he was alone at the dinner table.

He found himself waiting for…something else. That all-encompassing, unmistakable sense of magic he'd felt with the typhon earlier in the day. To be sure, the roaring was loud and startling, but as he spun around to take in the forest, looking for its source, the *absence* of fear was stark. Especially compared to earlier, when his entire body had been on edge. Now he was…well, perplexed more than anything.

"Psst! Peej!" Grant had cracked open the door from the safety of the tree house. "What are you doing? Come inside before you get squished!"

PJ rolled his eyes and walked over to the house, amused at Grant's white-faced fear, but didn't cross the threshold. "What happened to 'it's obviously not a real monster'?"

"Did you *hear* that?" Grant snapped, casting a

fearful look toward the trees. "And why are you all mellow? Shouldn't you be wetting your pants, too?"

PJ gave the canopy one final inspection then walked inside, closing the door behind him. "No, because I think I saw the real typhon earlier this evening."

Grant stared, dumbfounded, as PJ explained his trek into the forest earlier and coming basically face-to-face with the monster supposedly terrorizing the town.

"And you didn't think to tell me?" Grant snapped. "The townsfolk? Did you lead it to us?"

"No, because it wasn't interested in me. I could…sense it. It wanted to see me, and the forest wanted me to see it, but that was it." He gestured back toward the village. "That just now? That was something different. No magic, no sense, nothing that made me weak in the knees."

"That roaring didn't do it for you?" Grant said, grabbing the quilted blanket and wrapping it around himself. "Never heard anything so absolutely gut-wrenching in my entire life. And you're sitting there, Mr. Cool, like you weren't freaking out earlier in the day." He turned to PJ. "Was that the footprint we found, too?"

"You know… I don't know, really. It's possible, of course, but…" He pursed his lips, certainty settling in his stomach. "I think you're right.

Someone's doing a good job of trying to make us think it's a typhon."

"Yeah, well, they're doing too good a job," Grant muttered. "How are we gonna prove it?"

"You were on to something earlier. We have to get the truth about what Ellison is doing," PJ said. "Find out who else knows it, and who stands to gain if it doesn't happen. There's a whole village outside this forest who might be suspects, not to mention Harold—"

"I don't think any of those folks have the ability to do what we just heard, though," Grant said. "None of 'em are magical. They couldn't recreate a howling like that or make the earth move."

PJ had to concede that point. "People have secrets, and we only met them briefly. If we can get back out tomorrow, and Tim's able to talk to me again, I'll have him look at the folks a little more closely. But we should try to rest tonight, in any case. I don't think there's anything to worry about out there."

"You can't talk to Tim," Grant said pointedly. "How do you know?"

PJ opened and closed his mouth. He didn't have access to Tim, that was true, but in the absence of leaning on the dragon, he'd done pretty well with his own sense of magic. He hadn't needed Tim to sense the typhon approaching, or to feel that the footprint was an anomaly. And he hadn't needed Tim to assess that the dinner disrupter wasn't as terrifying as it sounded.

"I just know," PJ said, after a moment.

Grant eyed him. "Did you have some kind of epiphany out in the forest?"

"Maybe I'm just learning to trust my own gut as well as I trust Tim," PJ said, climbing into bed and pulling the quilt over himself. "Goodnight, Grant."

The rest of the night was uneventful, though PJ had dreams of inviting the typhon to the potluck, the massive creature sitting on one of the toadstools and sharing a tea with Hilde. It smiled at him, looking much less like a terrifying monster and more like a gentle giant, as it rose and walked away.

Bang…bang…bang…

That didn't sound right. The noise had been a thumping not a banging.

PJ woke bleary-eyed, forgetting for a moment where he was.

Bang. Bang. Bang.

He hadn't been dreaming the banging sound. And it was so urgent… Something terrible must've happened in the night. He leapt from the bed, but when he flung open the door, he jumped back in surprise.

It wasn't the typhon, or even one of the

townsfolk. No, *Harold* stood at the threshold of their small abode, carrying a bundle in his arms.

"W-what are you doing here?" was all PJ could stammer.

The gardener thrust the bundle into PJ's arms. "Mr. Thornhill figured you'd spent the night. Wanted to make sure you had what you needed."

PJ opened the bundle and realized the gardener had brought a set of sheets.

"That's kind of him, but it's the morning," PJ said, still trying to banish the last of the sleep fog from his mind. "We probably needed these last night, don't you think?"

Harold let out a *bah*. "Ungrateful. That's what you are. Probably magical like the rest of these freeloaders."

"We do appreciate it," PJ said with a plastered-on smile. "Seems like Ellison has Bill fixing up a lot of the houses around here, but Bill couldn't tell us why. Do you know?"

Harold's face darkened as he surveyed PJ. "You run into that typhon yet?"

PJ smirked at the abrupt change in subject. "We've seen some interesting things. There was another incident last night. We're actually headed back to town to ask Ellison about it."

Harold scoffed. "He won't know. Thinks he knows everything about this forest, but he ain't got a single clue. There's things in here that would sooner eat you than—"

"Yes, we're aware," PJ said. "But you clearly can walk to and from the forest, can't you? Have you been beyond the village?"

Harold's face shifted, as if he realized he'd inadvertently revealed something he shouldn't have. "The forest and me understand each other, yeah."

"So you can escort us out of the forest this morning, can't you?" PJ asked. "If you're headed back that way."

Harold's cheeks colored, and he grumbled but nodded. "I gotta unload all of *Mr. Thornhill's* supplies, then I'm headed back. But I ain't waiting for you, so you'd better be ready when I leave." With that, he huffed away, leaving PJ perplexed.

"You don't want to ask Ingrid to walk us out?" Grant was sitting up in bed, rubbing his face.

"I think we should try to pick Harold's brain," PJ said. "He obviously knows about the typhon, and the forest trusts him enough for him to come and go. Plus, I think he knows what Ellison is up to and might just tell us. He's clearly not that loyal to Ellison—"

"I don't know. Harold's doing his deliveries," Grant said, nodding to where the gardener was unloading items from the back of the wagon. "I don't know if you do that out of spite."

"Either way, he did agree to walk us out."

Grant peered out the window. "I don't think Harold's going to tell us much. He may not be loyal to Ellison, but he certainly doesn't like us. And I don't think Ellison's going to be forthcoming, either, since he hasn't been so far." He turned, casting a devious look at PJ. "We might just have to find the truth for ourselves."

PJ didn't like that look. "What are you thinking?"

"I mean, he's got that big house. Big houses probably have offices. Offices usually hold secrets."

PJ frowned. "We're not breaking into his mansion."

"Not break into, but..." Grant snapped his fingers. "We could ask him what literature he has about the typhon. All the snooty rich people houses have libraries with books they don't read. You saw what my Aunt Marion had back in Sheepsburg. I doubt she even knew what books were in there."

"And you think Ellison's going to let us just wander around his library?" PJ asked.

"I think he would, especially if we tell him we *saw* the typhon," Grant said. "And that we want to figure out how to ward the village from it. I think he'd gladly let us in his house for that. Then, we just figure some way to get him to leave us alone, and we'll go snooping."

"I don't love that idea," PJ said, glancing out the window. "It seems risky."

"We'll have Tim around to keep watch, since we'll be out of the forest," Grant said, wagging his eyebrows. "C'mon Peej, you know you want to find out what's really going on, don't you? If Ellison won't even tell *Bill* what he's got him doing all this work for, then he's not going to tell us until we confront him with proof."

"Fine." PJ huffed. "But only if we can ask Ellison first. Give him a chance to come clean."

"Pfft. You're no fun."

Harold made quick work of his deliveries, and, as he'd warned, he didn't even bother to look for the boys as he goaded the old mare back toward the forest. But PJ and Grant kept their distance so as not to raise the old man's ire.

"You'll be back, right?" Pat asked, catching up to them before they reached the edge of the enclave. "That monster didn't scare you off, did it?"

"Not yet," PJ said with a smile. "We're going to the village to get some answers. I hope. Be back before the sun goes down."

Pat smiled, and his black tongue fell out of his mouth. "Good. We're gonna try for another potluck tonight, and I'll be making my delicious roast chicken. Harold brought me three of 'em, and I've got a hankering."

PJ again promised they'd see all of them this afternoon then hurried to catch up with Grant and Harold. Once past the clearing, PJ waited for the forest to have a quarrel with them—perhaps push them back—but it seemed to sense that they were leaving and opened a path between the trees for the wagon to pass.

"So…" Grant started. "You come to the forest often?"

Harold grunted.

"How long have you worked for the Thornhills?" he tried again.

Another grunt.

"You must really love the magical folks in there."

That earned him a glare. "I do what I need to do to keep my job."

"We hear Ellison's getting light on gold," Grant continued. "Probably can't afford to pay you anymore."

"Do you need your ears cleaned, boy? I said I do what I need to keep my job." Harold faced forward in the seat, his shoulders tense.

Grant turned to PJ with a confused look, but PJ understood. "You aren't getting paid in gold, are you? Ellison's telling you to make these deliveries so you can continue to work at Thornhill Manor."

The gardener shifted.

"What's so important about the gardens there?" PJ asked.

"None of your business, that's what. I told you I'd bring you back to the village, not that I'd entertain a million questions." Harold slumped in the front seat of the wagon.

Grant opened his mouth, but PJ shook his head. The forest was coming to an end, and they'd have a chance to ask Ellison about his taciturn gardener. Besides that, PJ thought it *very* interesting that the man was so attached to a garden that he'd forego a paycheck, though he supposed that was a boon to the gold-strapped Ellison. But it did beg the question: what else might Harold do to keep his job there?

But all thoughts about Harold, the village, the typhon, and whatever else had been on the forefront of his mind evaporated when PJ stepped out from beneath the canopy and into the bright daylight of the morning. The pressure that had been squeezing his chest vanished, and a loud, welcome roar echoed between his ears.

That forest evil.

PJ let out a laugh of relief, clutching his chest. "Like actually evil or—?"

Keep me cage. No like.

Grant stopped walking when he realized PJ had as well, and Harold continued on to the village, ignoring them. "Tim's back already?"

PJ nodded. "What was it like for you, Tim?"

I not see much. Sleep lots. Typhon real.

"The typhon is real," PJ said, the nerves from seeing the monster in the forest coming back to the forefront.

Not bother village.

"But it's not the one threatening the village," PJ finished. "Like I thought."

Good gut. Follow. You know truth.

Pride blossomed in PJ's chest. Somehow, hearing he was fully capable of assessing a situation without his scaly sidekick made him feel ten feet tall.

"Why are you grinning?" Grant asked.

"No reason," PJ said.

You stupid take off amulet. Don't do again.

The grin fell from PJ's face. Of course there was going to be a lecture about that. "Sorry. I was desperate."

"What do you mean desperate?" Grant asked with a frown. "You know, it would be really nice if Tim would talk to me, too, sometimes."

The dragon reared up inside PJ, taking over his mouth and mind. *"PJ take off amulet in forest. Got stolen by raven."*

"I'm sorry, *what*?" Grant said, whirling on PJ. "Are you out of your mind?"

PJ, who couldn't defend himself while Tim was in charge, could only sit there.

"PJ scared. Thought necessary to talk. But need understand no need. PJ right. Typhon exist but no magic near village. Someone else trying to fool people. No need dragon to say that."

"Too right," Grant said. "Was this when you were out gallivanting in the forest?"

PJ finally wrested control back from Tim, exhaling and blinking away the magic in his eyes. "Yes. I only took it off for a second. I was actually hoping to call the grannies, but that darn bird swooped in and grabbed it."

"Must've been some bird," Grant said with a suspicious look.

"Look, the point is, I learned my lesson. No more taking it off around thieving fowls. And I'm going to trust my gut when it's clearly telling me something." PJ's face was burning—and not from the sun overhead. "So if we're done chastising me for something I already know, can we move on to what we're going to do?"

"Yes, yes," Grant said with a knowing smirk. "Off to sneak around Ellison's spooky old mansion."

Even though Forest Den was smaller and less populated, the village of Cheshireville was desolate in comparison. Knowing what he knew now, that everyone who lived there had moved to be in service to the mansion, he couldn't help but feel sorry for the folks who'd stayed. Thank goodness for the inn.

"Boys!" Roe and Oscar walked out of the bakery, carrying two custards in each hand. "Good to see you're still around! We didn't see you at the inn last night, so we worried all those *rumors* made you leave."

"No, we spent the night in Forest Den," PJ said,

nodding to the custards in their hands. "Those look delicious. We hadn't made it over to the bakery yet to try them ourselves."

"Here." Oscar offered the second of his. "But just be warned—they're addictive. You'll find yourself coming back to Cheshireville again and again."

PJ took the pastry. It was like a small pie, about the size of his palm, with a flaky crust and yellowy custard center that had several brown blisters on top. He broke it in half and handed the other piece to Grant, who popped it into his mouth without a second look.

"That's amazing," Grant said. "You aren't kidding about being addictive. I say we head to the bakery right now and get more, Peej."

PJ took a bite, and his mouth filled with the sweet, rich custard and buttery crust. He nodded to the two merchants approvingly. "Incredible."

"You'll have to pop in and tell Adonna about it," Roe said. "We're headed out this morning."

"Where are you going?" Grant asked.

"Our usual route," Oscar said. "We stayed an extra night last night because of a nasty storm that blew through. Did you guys see any of that?"

PJ shook his head. "It was dry in the forest."

"Ah, well, that place is strange, isn't it?" Roe said. "What about you boys? Are you headed out?

Solved the *mystery* of the typhon?"

"You know about that?" PJ asked, tilting his head.

"We know Harold's been ranting and raving about it," Oscar said. "And that Ellison scooped you up to investigate something in the forest. Assumptions were made at the inn last night. Lots of speculating, of course. I'm sure the townsfolk will be surprised to see you."

"We're headed to Ellison's now to talk about it," Grant said, his gaze suspicious. "But if you have any insights to share with us—"

"None at all," Roe said, holding up his hands. "But we do know Ellison is at the inn right now, *talking* with Kishan about those supplies Harold took into the forest. From what I understand, there's been a bit of miscommunication in order numbers."

"I'd give 'em a few minutes," Oscar said with a chuckle. "But we've got to hit the road before any more of the day gets away from us."

Roe nodded and shouldered his bag, "Have a good day, boys! Hopefully we'll see you around on our travels."

As they, too, didn't want to waste any more of the day, PJ and Grant headed to the inn to find Ellison. Neither he nor Kishan were in the front room, but there were raised voices coming from the back yard through the kitchen.

"I mean, Roe and Oscar did tell us to give them a minute," Grant said.

"Maybe we can break up the fight," PJ said. "C'mon."

They found the arguing pair just beyond the back door, surrounded by a mess of boxes and crates. Kishan stood to one side, his arms folded across his broad chest, and Ellison was off to the other, his cheeks rosy as he tried to pick up boxes.

"What's going on?" PJ asked.

"Ellison's manservant made a mess of my delivery," Kishan said tersely.

"He's not my..." Ellison sighed. "Nothing's damaged, is it? It all looks fine to me."

"You want me to tell that to the folks out there?" Kishan asked. "Brennan needed these new gears for his cider machine. He paid his last gold for them. And he's going to ask me why the crate is all scuffed up. And Adonna's glass has a nice new scratch on it. How is she supposed to use this to replace the one in her display case?"

"I'll...replace it," Ellison said with a grimace. "But I can't talk about this right now. Do you want to discuss the latest with the, erm, enclave?" He turned a hopeful smile on Grant and PJ. "You've got some answers, I hope? Did you get the delivery I sent with Harold?"

"This morning, yeah," PJ said.

Ellison scowled. "I told him… Never mind." He shook that off. "Shall we head somewhere more… private?" He cast a look at Kishan, who was picking up the crates while muttering about spoiled rich kids. "Or should we go back to the forest?"

"Let's go back to your house," PJ said.

Ellison seemed confused but more eager to get away from Kishan's ire than anything else, so he led them back toward the towering monstrosity he called a home. He didn't acknowledge them until they reached the tall iron gates around his mansion, and even then, all he did was glance behind him to make sure PJ and Grant were there. With a grunt, he pushed open the iron gate, which squeaked loudly and scraped against the cobblestone, just enough to be able to walk through. He stood on the other side and kept his hand on the gate.

"Harold insists I keep this closed," he said by way of explanation. "I'll get an earful if he finds it otherwise."

"Doesn't he work for you?" Grant asked, walking through.

"Harold's employment is…complicated," Ellison said with a sigh.

PJ followed, careful to avoid touching the iron, but once he was through, his gaze was drawn to the house. Up close, it was even more impressive. The bricks themselves had been imprinted with a design, and the windows were thick and shiny. The landscaping around the front was impeccable, with perfectly sculpted shrubs and evergreen trees that swayed in the breeze. A small fountain sat at the front of the house, though the water wasn't trickling today.

"He told us he's doing deliveries to the village so you'll let him keep working here," Grant said. "Which is odd, considering he seems to *hate* the people in Forest Den."

"That's a bit of an exaggeration," Ellison said, though he didn't quite meet their gazes. "He's just old and stubborn. I've asked him to retire at least seventeen times in the past three years—it's too much for him to keep up the whole house by himself. But he was the only one of my father's staff to refuse to leave. So he gets to keep tending to the grounds and I ask him to do a few errands here and there. The forest likes him, so he can do deliveries when I'm otherwise occupied."

PJ decided to leave that alone for the moment. "We've heard a lot about your father. What was he like?"

"The most social person you'd ever meet," Ellison said as he walked up the black marble steps to the looming, dark wooden doors. "In his time, this place was always humming with parties. Every night, practically, we were entertaining this person or that person from King's Capital. Lots of big names and bigger powers. Dreadful to try to get any sleep with magic shows happening just below your bedroom."

"Where did all his money come from?" Grant asked.

"That's rude," PJ muttered.

"It's a fair question," Ellison said, welcoming them inside. "I come from a long line of magical merchants, but Father made his money by cozying up to the most powerful witches and wizards in the king's court. Then, you know…" He sighed. "The queen came along, and the rest is history. He was arrested and…" He swallowed. "Well, I'm sure you can fill in the blanks."

PJ stood in the center of the foyer, which was cavernous but also showed its age. The sconces were empty, so the only light in the house came from the windows, which were dirtier than they looked from the outside. The paint on the wall was fading, and there was a light film of dust over everything. The walls did have impressively large paintings of what PJ assumed were Ellison's ancestors, but even they looked like they'd seen better days.

"Was your father magical?" Grant said, his hands on his hips as he took in the space.

"No, but he had a lot of powerful friends. So, by association..." He shrugged. "When my father was arrested, the queen's soldiers didn't know where to find all the gold he'd hidden. I was able to keep the servants on for a bit longer, but when one of my father's old friends showed up at my door, desperate and looking for sanctuary...that's when things changed." He walked toward the window that faced the forest. "When night fell, I helped him sneak into the forest, as I didn't have any other options. And to my surprise, the forest allowed him to come inside."

"You didn't think it would?" PJ asked.

"It's a temperamental thing," Ellison said. "It never hurt me as a boy, but I was certainly made aware when I strayed too far inside. But it welcomed that first person, then when more showed up, it welcomed those people, too. It was only supposed to be temporary." He chuckled. "Then one day, Bill met me at the edge and showed me what the forest had made for them. But while they had a lot, they didn't have everything they needed. That's when I knew I needed to step in. I contacted all my father's old nonmagical merchants and told them I was buying again—only this time, I'd be feeding the magicals next door."

"The queen's folks didn't pick up on that?" Grant asked.

"Oh, they certainly tried," Ellison said with a

laugh. "I might not have had my father's social graces, but I certainly had his brilliance. They knew I was doing something, but they couldn't ever prove it—and they couldn't find the magical folks, either." He nodded toward the forest. "When they went to the forest, it spat them back out. Literally."

"I'm sure they took that well," Grant said.

"They tried everything, even going so far as to try to burn it down, but the fire would never catch." Ellison smiled proudly. "Eventually, they just stopped trying. The townsfolk lived safely and secretly until the queen fell."

"Because of you," Grant said. "And all the money you spent. Continue to spend, in fact."

"It's the right thing to do," Ellison said. "My father had amassed a *lot* of gold, and I never… Gosh, I never really needed any of it. Better to help people who needed helping."

"And what about regular Cheshireville?" PJ asked. "You said you reached out to your father's old friends to supply what you needed but didn't ask the folks just outside your back door to help?"

"I didn't think they would be keen on helping, even if I'd asked Adonna to provide bread or Ulysses to send meat," Ellison said, his eyes darkening. "They were happy to entertain the queen's folks when they were trying to burn down the forest. I couldn't trust that they wouldn't tell the soldiers about any of it."

"Were they happy because they were loyal to the queen or because they finally had customers?" Grant asked.

Ellison flushed and looked like he'd rather not consider the alternative. "Erm. So what did you want to talk about?"

"We need access to your library," Grant said.

Ellison blinked. "My…library? Why?"

So he has one, PJ thought to himself. "Grant suspected you might have some literature that could help us ward the village against whatever's terrorizing it."

To PJ's surprise, Ellison nodded. "I couldn't save all the magical books, of course, but the ones I could, I hid in the forest until very recently. There's no telling what's in the crates, though. I can't guarantee it'll have what you're looking for."

"We'll take whatever you can give us," Grant said with a smile.

Ellison led them up a very fancy stairwell and down a hallway covered in paintings that glared down at the duo as if they knew they were doing wrong. PJ was just about to ask if the wall decor was magical, too, when Ellison stopped in front of a pair of double doors and opened them.

The library was just as large and impressive as the rest of the house, though not quite as big as the one at the university in Sheepsburg. Two magnificent floor-to-ceiling windows let the bright sunlight in. The walls of bookshelves stretched impossibly high toward the ceiling, and every single level was filled with books of all different sizes.

PJ spun around. "These are all yours, Ellison? You've read them all?"

"Oh, no," Ellison said with a chuckle. "No, no. I love books, don't get me wrong, and I've spent many afternoons lounging in here, hiding from my father's guests and losing myself in the world of knowledge. But even so, I've still only scratched the surface of what's here."

"Incredible," PJ said, walking to one of the stacks and glancing at the titles. *A History of Gardening. Different Kinds of Potatoes and Their Applications. A Complete History of Basket Weaving.*

"Oh, Hilde might like that one," Grant said, nodding to the last book PJ had touched.

"The magical books are over here," Ellison said, leading them to a stack of crates in the back of the library. "I pulled them out of the forest a few months ago, but I haven't had a chance to do anything with them." He shrugged. "I'd help, but I don't know the first thing about magic itself."

"Really? With all the magic that was around your father?" PJ asked.

"It wasn't an interest of mine," he said. "I care

about the people *with* magic, of course. But the power itself?" He shook his head. "Boring."

"You said it," Grant muttered, pulling the first book from the open stack. "At least these are more interesting. *Practical Potion-making* and *Spells and Sorcery: A Young Magical's Best Companion.*"

"Oh, I can put those away," Ellison said, taking them gently from Grant. "Unless you think these would be useful? Maybe practical potion-making?"

"Erm, we're not really brewers," PJ said with a nervous smile.

Ellison took the books to the other side of the library, leaving Grant to mime something PJ couldn't decipher.

PJ mimed something back, but Grant didn't seem to understand, either.

But Ellison was walking back, so PJ began pulling more books from the box.

"Boy, this is gonna take a while," Grant said, almost a little too loudly. "Do you think you could rustle us up a cuppa? Might give us the stamina to get through all these boring books."

PJ pulled an encyclopedia of magical creatures from the crate next, which might actually come in handy, so he put that aside. "I agree."

"Oh, right. That's what people do when they host, isn't it?" Ellison said, rubbing the back of his head. "Sorry, I'm not sure... Let me run down to the kitchen and see what I've got. Or maybe Harold's got something. Are you two going to be okay in here by yourselves?"

"Absolutely," Grant said with an overly cheery smile. "Take your time. We'll probably be a while."

CHAPTER ELEVEN

Grant silently counted down from five fingers then walked to the door and peered out. "Okay, he's gone. C'mon, I saw an office down the hall."

"This isn't a good plan," PJ said. "Why don't we stay in here and—"

"We'll be quick," Grant said. "And keep yer voice down. I don't want that grumpy gardener overhearing us. He'd sooner run us through with his rake than speak to us."

I keep watch.

PJ scowled, a little annoyed his dragon was taking Grant's side but grateful for the help. "Okay. Just actually *be* quick."

They tiptoed down the hall, PJ ducking as he made eye contact with one of the paintings. The eyes seemed to follow him as he passed, and he once again wondered if they were enchanted.

"Are we almost there?" PJ whispered, giving one painting with a particularly disgruntled man wearing a full suit of armor a once-over. "I'm getting creeped out."

"Couldn't kill him to light a candle or two, could it?" Grant whispered back. "Downright dreary."

"I'm sure that's what those servants he let go did all day," PJ said, passing by a sconce covered in cobwebs. "As well as clean up a bit."

"Yeah, this place is filthy," Grant replied. "I mean, what's the point of having this big house if you aren't going to keep it up?" He tapped his nose. "Another point for the side of 'he's trying to make his money back.'"

PJ didn't argue, as he was unnerved by a painting of a man fighting what appeared to be a three-headed dog—and the dog was winning. He bumped into the back of Grant, who'd stopped at one of the doors to peer inside.

"Not this one."

"Wait," PJ frowned, "you said you saw an office on the way in."

"Well, not with Ellison just now," Grant said,

opening another door. "I mean, I saw it when we first came by the manor."

PJ balled his fists, swallowing all manner of curses in order to stay quiet. "*Grant,*" he whispered harshly. "We can't just wander around aimlessly."

"I definitely think that's what we're doing." He opened another door. "Another bedroom. Who needs all these bedrooms?"

"Someone's going to see us," PJ said, looking behind him to where a woman with a curled lip and a jeweled scepter watched him with wide dark eyes from a gilded painting. "I think someone's already seen us."

Grant took a left at the next bend in the hallway, and PJ, torn between returning to the library and staying with his friend to keep him out of trouble, begrudgingly followed. It was another long stretch of doorways with only a scant amount of light from a single, filthy window.

"You could make this quicker by helping, you know," Grant said, peering inside another room.

"How?" PJ scowled and opened another door before a tail *thwapped* loudly in his mind. "Right, yes, please."

Tim sped ahead of them, peering into each of the doors down this hall and the one around the corner until he stopped at a large double door in the center of the hallway. Beyond that was exactly the office Grant had been describing.

"Well, why didn't he do that before?" Grant said when PJ told him.

They ran as quietly as they could toward the doors PJ had seen in his mind's eye, pushing them open and pausing in the entryway. The room was half the size of the library but still quite impressive. There were again floor-to-ceiling windows, though this time, they overlooked the perfectly manicured garden in the back, along with an expansive, wooden desk with a single chair facing out. There were stacks of paper on top, and what appeared to be a cold cup of tea. So clearly Ellison had been in here recently.

"C'mon," Grant said, ushering PJ inside and closing the door behind him. "Let's see what we can find."

There were, unsurprisingly, unpaid invoices on the desk for all the food and supplies Ellison had purchased for the Forest Den townsfolk. Based on what PJ could understand of them, his accounts were in good standing with all his vendors, which meant he probably wasn't in danger of going bankrupt. But the gold owed was still a staggering amount, more than PJ's parents made in three years as farriers.

"Find anything yet?" Grant asked, rifling through the papers inside the desk.

"Only that I grew up very poor," PJ said, putting the invoices back the way he'd found them. "Oh, wait, look at this. I think it's a letter from King's Capital."

PJ carefully unfolded the already unsealed letter and read.

Dear Ellison,

I do apologize for the delay in returning your letter. Things are chaotic here in King's Capital still, as we find ourselves quite busy undoing the damage Meandra caused and quelling the fires as they arise. As I'm sure you can guess, we've been slow to rebuild our military might, trying to sort through who's on which side from the soldiers claiming loyalty.

That being said, we finally seem to have a handle on the new fires and can focus our attention on some older ones. I'm leading a contingent of soldiers near your home to locate an artifact we've been missing for a long time. I'd be happy to stop in and see what you've been doing in the forest.

Yours,
Andres Rade

"Why does that name sound familiar?" PJ asked. "Andres Rade."

"I dunno. Maybe you read about him in a book somewhere," Grant replied. "When was that letter dated?"

"Three weeks ago." PJ glanced at the top of the letter. "Right around—"

"The time the monster noises started," Grant finished, grinning. "That's a clue if ever I saw one."

"I wonder what kinda artifact he's looking for," PJ murmured. "Do you think it's somewhere in Ellison's house? He said his father was friends with lots of powerful people."

"Who knows?" Grant said, pulling books off the shelf to flip through them. He closed the book and put it back. "Maybe we should reach out to the grannies again. They seem to know people in King's Capital. They could tell us who this Andres guy was."

"Do you think they're back in their human forms?" PJ asked. "They wrote a letter to help the Padstow kids. I wonder if that was a one-off, or...?"

"Maybe they flew to King's Capital in their dragon forms," Grant said with a snort. "And scared the pants off everyone there. That Andres fellow did say they were 'quelling pop-up fires.'" He wagged his brows. "Maybe they're dragon-caused."

"I don't think the grannies would be that careless," PJ said, though he couldn't hold in a smile.

Focus.

"Right." PJ turned away from the desk, scanning the office for anything else interesting when he spotted movement in the garden. He took one step toward the window when Tim stopped him.

You stay. I listen.

The dragon unfurled its wings in PJ's mind and flew through the window (mentally, of course), doing a quick spin in the air to stretch out before diving back down to where PJ had seen the movement. Ellison was arguing with Harold, who wore a wide-brimmed hat and was pointing his rake threateningly at his boss.

"...a lot of nerve, doing this! You know it's not right."

"If you don't like it," Ellison said, ignoring the de facto weapon pointed near his face, "you can leave."

"I ain't gonna leave, boy. I made a promise that I'd keep this garden, and I intend to keep it." He sniffed. "And don't you dare try to fire me, cause I got keys. And you'd never be able to get back inside your fancy little house."

"I'm not going to fire you, Harold," Ellison said patiently. "But you do need to get with the times. This is happening. And if you don't like it—"

"Aye, we'll see what that forest thinks of your grand plans," Harold said with a devilish smile. "Wouldn't it be interesting if that monster everyone's talking about knocks over all them tree houses?"

"That's not... There is no monster." Ellison sighed. "Just some overactive imaginations."

"That's not what I hear," Harold said. "Those interlopers in the forest keep leaving because of it. Hard to believe they'd be afraid of something that's the same as they are."

"They're going home, not running scared," Ellison said, though it was clear from the redness on his cheeks that he was lying. "And I'd appreciate it if you'd quit spreading nasty rumors to everyone in town about it, too. I now have a pair of magical investigators in my library because you opened your big mouth to Kishan at the inn."

"They're just a couple-a boys. Sure they aren't

taking you for a ride?" Harold smirked. "You are awfully gullible."

Ellison bristled. "I'm not gullible, and I'm not paying them. In fact, they never actually asked for compensation."

"Maybe they're the ones making all the ruckus, hopin' you'll cough up some gold," Harold said. "But what do I know? I'm just an old gardener. You're a *learned man*. I'm sure you know what you're doing." He chuckled, turning to walk away. "I bet those boys are stealing whatever's left of your good silver. Mark my words—they aren't who they say they are."

"They're right in the library, as they're supposed to be," Ellison said, though he didn't sound too confident about that.

"Are you *sure*?"

The gardener turned, and PJ swore he looked right *at* him.

"Quite. I'll head there now just to check on them," Ellison said, turning on his heel. "And I'm sure they've found… Well, they've found exactly what they're looking for."

PJ sucked Tim back into his body and turned to Grant. "We gotta get back to the library. Now."

~

Grant put back what he'd found, scowling, and together, they let Tim lead them right back to the library (they'd clearly taken the long way, because it was just around the corner). Once inside, Grant headed to the stack of books, but PJ snagged the encyclopedia he'd put aside. He thumbed through the first few pages until he landed on the first creature. There was a short paragraph about it along with an ink drawing. It looked rather jovial as it danced amongst the drawn-on flowers. The next page showed a creature that was the complete opposite, with long fangs and claws, who growled menacingly back at PJ.

He mindlessly flipped through the pages, keeping his gaze on the door, when his fingers felt something strange on the edge of the paper. The corner of the page had been folded down, and the page itself had a drawing of a dog running through the fields, looking to be mid-bark. It had floppy ears and a wide grin and seemed very familiar.

"Huh."

"What?" Grant asked. "Did you actually find something?"

"Not related to Forest Den, but I think I figured out why Bev's dog always seemed so strange to me," PJ said, looking down at the creature known for sniffing out magic. "Laelaps. It's a magical detector."

"Bev had a laelaps?" Grant turned the book toward himself and read the description. "It says they're only attracted to powerful wizards. She's not a powerful wizard…is she?"

But PJ's gaze drew to the creature on the facing page. "Lakanica. A nymph of the spirit and meadows with the ability to create springs in the earth. Blue hair and skin." He turned up to Grant. "Delaney and Audra."

"And?"

"This page was bookmarked," PJ said, turning the book on its side. More pages were dog-eared, too. He flipped to another page in the front, revealing a half-man, half-deer. "Here's Bill, the centaur. And look…" He flipped to the next one a few pages over, which had a dog-headed man. "Pat. He's a cyancephalic."

"That's a name," Grant said. "I think I prefer Pat."

He flipped to the next one, where he found the description of a dryad—Ingrid. Going further, he spotted creature descriptions for more of the folks in town, including Hilde the chepi, and more creatures who must've already moved on.

"Maybe Ellison was just trying to find out what they all are?" Grant said. "I don't—"

But as PJ turned to one of the last dog-eared pages, his frown deepened.

TYPHON

The typhon is one of the largest creatures in existence. Exceedingly rare, they can live hundreds, if not thousands, of years and can be found in mountains, large forests, and other places where they can remain hidden. Their numbers dwindled after it was discovered that their hearts could be turned into pure magic, and so they tend to avoid other creatures where possible. Although their size and amount of magic might be frightening to those who can sense it, they're generally peaceful.

The picture was a large man-like creature with a tall tree to show its height. It was bald, with a wrinkled face, an overly large nose, and a kind smile. Its hands swung down at its hips and looked almost too big for its body, and its feet were bare.

"It looks kinda…sweet?" Grant said, tilting his head. "Are we sure this is the thing you saw?"

Their conversation was cut short when Ellison walked through the doors, carrying a tray with a kettle and three cups. "Sorry about the delay. Had to deal with some gardening issues with Harold. I can make you more if it's too cold."

"It'll be just fine," PJ said, trying hard to keep his face neutral. "Harold does a good job with the garden. From what I've seen of it, that is."

"He's a great gardener, but a terrible employee," Ellison said with a sigh. "I do feel for him. I think this place is as close to a family as he's ever had, and he couldn't survive without it. We mostly avoid each other, to be honest." He nodded toward the book. "Did you find anything interesting?"

"Noticed you'd dog-eared the pages," PJ said. "For some of the creatures you encountered in the forest."

Ellison's brows creased. "Dog-eared? I would never. That thing's old and expensive…" He crossed the room and licked his lips as PJ showed him the page with the centaur on it. "That's strange. I didn't do that."

"You said you'd hidden these books in the forest, right?" PJ asked.

"I did." He frowned as he straightened the page. "Look at it. The page is all wrinkled. I wonder if it'll come out."

"I mention it because…" PJ flipped to the page with the typhon.

Ellison paled. "That's… I've never seen anything like that in the forest. Are you sure?"

"I saw it yesterday," PJ said pointedly. "The real

thing, but I'm not sure that it's what we're looking for."

"What do you mean?" Ellison asked, glancing nervously out the window.

"We think someone's trying to stir up trouble to scare the townsfolk into leaving," Grant interjected coolly, watching Ellison with a sharklike expression.

"Why would someone want to do that?" Ellison asked, sounding genuinely upset. "Haven't these people suffered enough? They lost their homes—twice, in some cases—and they've finally found a community where they can thrive. Who would want them to leave?"

PJ and Grant gave each other a look. "Well, you," Grant said.

"Me?" Ellison took several steps back. "Why would I want to—"

"You've got Bill renovating the vacant houses," PJ said. "To sell them."

"I'm not going to… I'm not *selling* them! I'm trying to revitalize the community," Ellison said, sinking down into his seat. "By turning it into a magical tourist destination."

Chapter Twelve

Magical tourist destination.

PJ repeated the words in his mind. They made sense apart, but together, his brain couldn't comprehend the concept.

"Look, there's been a lot of change over the past few years," Ellison said. "First, magic was good. Then it was bad. Then it was good again. I'd really like a chance to show people—especially those who may never have seen any kind of magic—that the ones who do have it are normal folk."

"By making them perform like traveling bards?" Grant asked with a quirked brow.

"Not perform, no." Ellison shook his head. "They'd just do what they normally do. Hilde can weave her baskets. The Jerichos could continue to dredge up new wellsprings from the ground. Bill could do his woodworking. Ingrid could show how she communicates with the trees. Melinda could sell her crystals with small magics. But instead of, well, relying on *me* to pay for food and whatnot, we charge the tourists."

"And you profit," Grant said.

"Only enough to cover my expenses," Ellison said, with a small smile. "An administrative fee, if you will, for handling the advertising and the like. Unfortunately, the king does still demand taxes, and I *may* have spent a little more than I should've on feeding the folks in Forest Den. I'm sure you noticed the state of the house."

"You could sell your house if you're strapped for gold," Grant said. "It's pretty big. I bet you could get a lot for it."

"Well, that's..." He sighed. "That's Plan B. If this holiday town doesn't happen. But don't mention *that* to anyone in Forest Den, lest they think I'm abandoning them."

"Maybe that's for the best, though," PJ said. "They don't have to stick around if they can't support themselves. And you don't have to be the one to keep things running."

"Yes, but..." His face brightened as he clasped his hands together. "Could you imagine? A steady stream of new people coming to this wonderful town we've built. Paying gold just to be amongst these incredible people. And no one has to leave."

"Okay, so if everyone supposedly benefits from Plan A, where you set up this tourist destination," PJ asked, "why doesn't anyone in Forest Den know about it? Even Bill doesn't seem to know why he's building furniture for these vacant houses."

"To be honest...I was about to tell them. I didn't want to get everyone excited until I'd sorted everything out, and I'd just gotten news from a potential investor that he was planning to come. Then..."

"Then the monster showed up," PJ said with a nod.

He shook his head. "Seven years of peace, and this typhon decides to terrorize the village *now*. I've got the worst luck."

"Or someone's out to sabotage you," Grant said. "And put a stop to this holiday tourist town."

Ellison frowned as if he hadn't even considered that possibility. "No, it's not... I don't think..." His cheeks grew rosy. "Who'd want to do that?"

PJ and Grant again stared at each other. Was he that innocent? Or was he still hiding something?

"There's a whole group of townsfolk in

Cheshireville who might want to, especially with the way you treated them after your father was arrested," PJ said.

"They haven't a clue about what I'm doing," he said, shifting uncomfortably. "And to be honest, I… Well, I rather assume they'll be packing up and leaving once they hear of all the magical folks who'll be parading through."

"They hate magical folks that much?" Grant asked. "Enough to leave the town they love?"

"I honestly don't know," he said, color darkening his cheeks. "They won't speak to me, and I don't speak to them if I can help it. But they don't play into my plans. They don't even know what's going on in Forest Den."

"They know more than you think, thanks to Harold," Grant said. "When we first got to town, we had dinner at the inn, and everyone seemed to know that something was scaring the forest folks into leaving."

"Harold even mentioned the typhon," PJ said.

"Kishan knew because a few of the folks who'd been scared out of Forest Den stopped by his inn," Ellison said. "And Harold just likes to be mean to people. But those people have never actually been allowed inside the forest, so I don't see how they could be responsible for scaring everyone."

"Have you considered the *forest* might not want

you to turn it into a magical holiday spot?" Grant asked. He gestured to PJ. "I mean, Peej and I can't walk in without an escort."

"I already worked that out with Ingrid," Ellison said. "She assures me—"

"Ingrid can't control all the trees," Grant said.

"She told me the ones along the path are quite agreeable," he said. "And I've never had a problem. I'm sure there will have to be some conversations with the trees—assurances made that the tourists will stay in the village—but I don't think there'll be a problem."

"You know, I'm not sure the forest is our problem, actually," PJ said to Grant. "It sort of... told me so when I asked."

"You can talk to the forest?" Ellison asked, eyes wide.

"Kind of," PJ said. "It still doesn't trust me. And my dragon isn't able to speak to me while we're inside at all. So that's something to consider as you advertise the forest to others."

"On the contrary, I think that might be a selling point," Ellison said with a brief smile. "No need to fear powerful wizards while you're on holiday. Everyone's magic will be kept to a minimum." He chuckled. "If we can even get this thing moving, with the monster as it is."

"We have a few hours before sundown," PJ said

to Grant. "I'd like to talk with Kishan and the others about what kind of rumors are flying around town, and we'll need to get back before it gets dark. If we're going to catch this person, we need to be in Forest Den."

"I agree," Grant said. "But how are we gonna get back there later? It's not exactly letting us come and go."

"I can escort you later this afternoon," Ellison said with a half-smile. "I'm expecting another shipment of supplies for the townsfolk, and, erm, Harold was quite clear that he's not making any more trips today. What do you say we meet at the inn around five?"

With their plan set, Ellison walked them to the front gates, effectively circumventing any further attempts to snoop more around the house. He once again pleaded with them to use their discretion when talking with the townsfolk, which just served to make PJ more suspicious.

While the distance to the village was short, the boys took a long walk toward the green fields to discuss the events of the past few hours in private.

"So we've got our motive," Grant said. "Who are our suspects?"

"Anyone who stands to gain from Ellison *not* creating his holiday spot," PJ said. "Cheshireville folks might not want to have more magical folks around. If any of them know about the holiday spot, that's pretty incriminating."

"Agreed," Grant said. "Could also be someone in Forest Den, like we thought earlier. Someone who doesn't want all those people to come. Like Hilde."

"Very good chance," PJ said. "And if someone's hiding some extra magic the rest of the town doesn't know about, that could explain how they've been able to fool everyone."

"And we're pretty sure it's not the forest?" Grant said. "Those trees wouldn't talk to Ingrid around that footprint."

"Yeah, that was really strange," PJ said. "And strange that the forest wanted me to see the typhon, too."

"You think it wanted you to see it?"

"It literally opened a pathway from me to him," PJ said. "Then once we saw each other, it closed and led me back to the village."

"Was this before or after you stupidly removed your amulet?"

PJ ignored him. "If we're going to focus our attention on Cheshireville, we need to think about *how* they'd do it. They hadn't been allowed in the forest—"

"So they say," Grant said. "Could be lying."

PJ arranged the puzzle pieces in his mind, but they didn't seem to fit together. "What do you make of that letter we found? That Andres guy said he was coming to check out the forest."

"Do you think someone intercepted it, and that's why they started all the ruckus?" Grant asked.

"Could be," PJ said. "Who'd have access to Ellison's mail? Harold?" He shook his head. "Unless *he's* hiding some magical abilities, I don't think he's our culprit. There's no way he could've made all that noise."

"I'll remind you that Valta and I distracted a highly intelligent magic hunter with a floating lantern, some loud noises, and good luck," Grant said.

"True."

"You know, there are more holes in Ellison's holiday plan than there are trees in the forest," Grant said. "I mean, why do you think he's not telling anyone? You think it's really because he doesn't want to get their hopes up?"

Ellison was a man who seemed uninterested in money, and very uninterested in power. Perhaps someone who'd been taken advantage of a little by the magical folks who stayed behind. But those magical folks were nothing if not loyal to him.

Still, that loyalty might be tested if they found out what his plans were.

Ellison naive came Tim's assessment.

"Be more subtle, why don't you?" Grant said when PJ told him. "You think someone can *be* that naive? Or am I just jaded after months on the road?"

"It's been less than a month since we left Sheepsburg." PJ rolled his eyes.

"Fine. But still. I can't imagine going through life so gullible." Grant turned back to the mansion. "Then again, if I had all that money, maybe I'd be that naively optimistic, too."

PJ didn't disagree, but they weren't getting any answers out here on the plains. "Who do you want to talk with first?"

"The baker, obviously," Grant said with a firm nod.

"You just want another custard."

"Well?" He chuckled. "If they bring Oscar and Roe off the beaten path, why can't I want another one?"

PJ didn't disagree, because he, too, wanted another one, so they headed toward the small bakery. It was a neat building made of brick, with a large window out front. As PJ entered, he was met by the scent of sugar, flour, and butter. It smelled heavenly to him, but Grant made a face.

"Reminds me of Allen's bakery back home," he said with a shake of his head.

"Those cookie-making skills of yours have come

in handy," PJ said, walking up to the glass shelf showing an assortment of custards like Roe and Oscar had shared with them. "Though I can't say I ever saw Allen bake something like this. I wonder how she makes them?"

"You know, the way Roe and Oscar were raving about these, I bet it could help Ellison with his holiday spot, too," Grant said. "Come for the magicals, stay for the custards! I can see it now. Flyers all over the place. Lines out the door. That sort of thing."

PJ nodded. "It's rather strange that Ellison hasn't even tried to approach them with a business deal. You'd think they'd be over the moon to have more folks coming to their door."

"He does think they hate magical things," Grant said.

"Goodness, customers!" Adonna came rushing out of the back, looking quite flustered. She quickly pulled off a flour-covered apron and flashed them the brightest smile she could. "Welcome to Adonna's Delights! I'm Adonna. What can I get for you two— Wait... You're the duo who's been helping Ellison, aren't you?" Her formerly cheery expression darkened considerably, and she seemed to be rethinking the custards she was plating. "That'll be three silvers."

"Three silvers? For two small custards?" Grant

started but PJ waved him off.

"Happy to support a local business." Of course, the amulet ensured he had it in his pocket, so it really didn't bother him too much. "Roe and Oscar shared one of the custards with us before they left this morning. They were so good we had to come by."

"Mm." She swiped the silvers off the counter and took a large step back. "What kinda magical are you, anyway?"

PJ cleared his throat as Grant snorted. "Pardon?"

"I mean, when the forest first opened, I saw all kinds of things. Big creatures, little creatures, and ones that looked more or less human. Brennan next door told me those were the ones to worry about. Human-looking creatures were the ones with the most hidden magic, so..." She nodded at PJ. "What kinda creature are you? If you're able to go to and from the forest."

"I'm a run-of-the-mill human," Grant said with a charming smile. "You know, you don't have to be magical to stay in the forest. It's quite lovely for those of us without any of it at all."

She wasn't swayed by the change of subject, turning to PJ. "And you?"

"Magical investigator," he said, instead of the whole truth. Somehow, he got the sense she'd break out a pitchfork if he told her about Tim. "We're actually looking into who's causing trouble in the magical village. Lots of folks are really scared in there."

She blew air between her lips. "Classic Ellison. He'll give everyone else a gold coin before he gives us a second look. It's a good thing Kishan came when he did. I think he took pity on us, to be honest. Wasn't easy for him to get that inn up and running. We all had to chip in. And meanwhile, Ellison's just sitting up there with all his money and didn't contribute his time or his money or anything."

"I can certainly see how you'd think he abandoned you," PJ said, trying to sound as neutral as possible. "But he was helping those in the forest. They probably needed it more than you."

She scoffed. "Well, we were in the lurch just the same as them—though probably we were worse off. As we told you the other day, Kishan is the reason I'm still in business. Him and those merchants. It's thanks to them that I've got customers from here to the southern peninsula." She paused, beaming. "They're good people. Glad Kishan brought them here when he did."

"They're friends of Kishan's?" PJ asked.

She nodded. "I think they all used to travel together," she said. "Or maybe he met them when he was a traveling magician."

PJ blinked. "A traveling…what? Magician?"

"I thought he was an entertainer," Grant said. "Like a bard?"

"How did he escape the queen?" PJ asked.

"Oh, he's not a *real* magic user, mind you. Just the kind that could disappear a rabbit with sleight of hand or use smoke and mirrors to put on a show," she said. "I think that's why he was in such high demand at Thornhill Manor. Anyone with real magic was boring, but a nonmagical person who could fool a wizard into thinking he could walk through walls?" She shook her head. "They couldn't get enough of him."

"Interesting," Grant said, rubbing his chin as he met PJ's gaze. An entertainer like that would certainly be capable of putting on a show to scare innocent townsfolk. "What other sorts of feats did he do?"

"Not sure," she said with a small shrug. "I didn't work at the house too much. But Brennan—he owns the cidery next door—he used to work there. He could probably tell you more." She wiped her hands on her apron and inched backward toward the back door of the kitchen. "If that's all, I've got bread baking in the oven…"

Chapter Thirteen

Sensing they'd gotten all they could from the baker, the boys took their pastries and ate them outside. Grant gobbled his in two bites while PJ savored his, eyeing the inn across the street. It was interesting that Kishan never mentioned his background as a magician, only calling himself an entertainer. Was he trying to avoid suspicion? Or maybe, to Kishan, an entertainer and a magician were interchangeable terms.

They headed to the cidery, where they were met by a different set of aromas, this time of fermentation, sweet apples, and old wood. There wasn't much to the shop, just a single room filled with barrels tilted on their sides, all marked with dates. There was also a cider press, and next to that, several large crates of apples that looked like they were ready to be pressed.

"Think he'll let us get another sample?" Grant asked with a knowing grin as he walked over to one of the barrels. "I don't think we're going to be dining at the inn any time soon."

"Can I help you?" Brennan poked his head in from outside and, as with Adonna, his face fell when he recognized them. "I'm not selling any cider to Ellison, so you two can turn around and leave right now."

PJ and Grant shared a look. "We're not here for that," PJ said.

"But that's an interesting way to greet us," Grant said, plastering on his cheesy, pleasant smile. "Ellison hired us to look into some trouble happening in Forest Den."

Brennan snorted. "What kinda trouble?"

"The kind that's scaring the folks out of their homes," PJ said.

"Good riddance," Brennan said with a shake of his head. "That forest is strange enough without all of them living there and making it stranger."

"You said you were a manservant at Thornhill Manor, right?" Grant asked. "How'd you end up with the cidery?"

"Happened into it," he said, watching them suspiciously. "The old owner didn't have any family, but we got along pretty good. Worked with him a lot as I was one of Marley Thornhill's gopher boys in the house. Would always be coming and going to get him whatever he needed to make his guests happy. When the old cidery owner told me he was gonna retire, he offered to sell it to me. And things were good, for about a year. I'm just lucky I was able to pay the old man back before everything went sideways."

"When the queen's soldiers arrested Ellison's father," PJ said.

Brennan nodded. "It was a rough few months. Went from selling five barrels a night to having to drive around in my wagon, begging tavern owners to take some off my hands. Then Kishan showed up." He sighed. "Took over the inn and suddenly we had people moving through town again. Met some travelers with friends in nearby cities and was able to get some steady business. Kishan buys a cask about once a week. I'm not back to where I was before, but at least I'm able to feed myself."

PJ nodded. He was starting to get a sense for why Ellison had avoided the Cheshireville set, but at the same time, he could see a very easy solution. If Ellison's holiday spot got off the ground and a steady stream of magical folks were coming and going, then maybe Brennan could get back to selling five barrels a night.

"Look," Brennan shifted, "I'm sorry for what's happening to the folks in Forest Den. I know they've been through a lot, and I actually do think it was nice of Ellison to spend his money helping them. But I also think they've gotten too comfortable in there. Now, we hear Ellison's thinking of selling his house—"

"Who told you that?" PJ asked.

"Harold," Brennan said. "Apparently, he saw something in Ellison's office the other day. Ranted and raved about it."

"Would you mind if he sold his house?" Grant asked.

He shrugged. "I don't care what he does. His manor may loom over us, but we've built separate worlds. He does his thing with the forest folk. We do ours out here to support Kishan's inn."

"We were actually curious about Kishan and his history," Grant said. "Adonna told us you saw a lot of Kishan's magic in action."

"It's not magic-magic," he said, almost a little too quickly. "It's smoke and mirrors, mostly. Obviously, he and the rest of us were tested by the queen, and if they'd found anything, they would've taken him away." He tilted his head. "Why do you ask?"

"We've got a theory that someone's doing their best to disrupt Ellison's plans for the forest," Grant said, thankfully being vague. "And that disruption looks like something a magician or the like would do."

"Kishan wouldn't hurt a fly," Brennan said, his face contorting into a scowl. "He's a good innkeeper, and a good soul. Adonna and I owe everything to him, I..." He stopped, clicking his tongue. "But if you're looking for someone with a vendetta against Ellison *and* the forest folks, talk to Harold. I'd bet you a whole bushel of apples he's the one behind it."

"He's not hiding any special abilities, is he?" PJ asked.

"No, but he hates the forest folk about as much as he hates Ellison," Brennan said. "I mean, I've known the man since I was a boy, and he's always been mean to everyone except his plants. But something snapped in him when all those magical things started leaving the forest. Then, when he found out Ellison had been helping them?" He shook his head. "I'm surprised Ellison hasn't been smothered to death by his own pillow. I certainly wouldn't want someone with keys to my house that angry with me. Then again, Harold complains about everything, so maybe Ellison doesn't see it."

"What else does Harold complain about?" PJ

asked.

"Take your pick," Brennan said. "The weather, the way Adonna does her custards, the way the butcher cuts the meat, the way Ellison pays him, the way Ellison talks, Ellison in general, the magical folks, how the magical folks walked too close to the manor when they were leaving, the way Ellison's obsessed with them instead of the nonmagical folks out here…" He sighed. "It's exhausting."

"Has he mentioned anything about Ellison's plans for the forest?" PJ asked. "Other than trying to sell the house?"

Brennan shook his head. "Mostly going on about that typhon to strangers, like yourself. It's easy to laugh off if you're avoiding the forest, like most travelers are. I don't think anyone's going to willingly go there. Goodness knows it told us to steer clear, and we're all going to listen."

"Back to Kishan—" Grant started, but Brennan shook his head.

"If you have a question for Kishan, go ask him yourself. He's got nothing to hide from anyone. Least of all two magical investigators." Brennan crossed his arms over his chest. "And I'm not in the habit of spreading gossip about the one man in this town who cares about us. So unless you're going to buy a cask of cider, I suggest you leave."

"I think this town oughta be bigger," Grant said as they walked the twenty steps to the inn. "Amazing how much animosity can build in such a confined area."

They walked into the inn, which was unsurprisingly quiet for mid-afternoon. The innkeeper wasn't at his post—but a quick search found him in the backyard chopping wood.

"You're back," Kishan said with a tight smile. "Did Ellison bore you to tears?"

"A little," PJ said. "We actually had a few questions for you, if you've got some time."

Kishan turned to them, suspicion flitting across his face as he put the axe down. "Sure. What's up? Still investigating the mystery in the forest?"

"We are," PJ said. "And we're pretty sure it's not a typhon."

"Don't tell Harold," Kishan said with a laugh. "He'll be heartbroken to hear his bedtime story isn't resonating anymore."

"We think it might be someone out to sabotage Ellison," Grant said.

Kishan shifted, almost imperceptibly. "Ellison does enough to sabotage himself."

"So we hear, but..." PJ tilted his head. "He's trying to recoup some of the gold he spent on the folks in the forest. Has a new business plan that features Forest Den as its centerpiece."

"So you've come to talk to me about it?" Kishan asked with a quirked brow. "Why?"

"You seem to know what's going on in the village," PJ said. "Figured we'd talk to you about it and see what you might've heard in the dining room."

"I do hear a lot," he said, picking up the axe and swinging it. "But other than Harold complaining about Ellison selling his house, I haven't heard anything about his plans, least of all about Forest Den."

PJ waited for him to say more, but he just kept chopping the wood.

"What's your opinion on the folks who live in Forest Den?" Grant asked, after a long pause.

He chuckled. "They don't bother me. I spent a lot of time at Thornhill Manor in its heyday, so I saw a lot of different kinds of creatures. Mages, wizards, centaurs, men with spiders for heads. Really didn't faze me too much."

"Because you're magical yourself?" Grant asked.

Kishan's smile widened. "Magic*ian*, not magic*al*."

"What's the difference?" PJ asked, feigning ignorance. "You told us you were an entertainer."

"A magician *is* an entertainer," he said with a hearty chuckle. "I was all the rage at Thornhill Manor precisely because I could do magnificent tricks without a drop of actual magic in my veins. You should've seen the wizards and how their eyes fell out of their head when a pathetic nonmagical could make them disbelieve their own eyes. They begged me to tell them how I did it, but of course, I'd never reveal my secrets." Pride flashed on his face.

"Then you decided to hang it up," PJ said.

"You two are young, still, but after a while, traveling wears on you. I wanted to settle somewhere quiet."

"Couldn't have picked a quieter town," Grant said. "Except in the past three weeks, when that monster's been terrorizing the Forest Den folks."

"Well, thankfully, that stays over there," Kishan said. "But you said it wasn't a typhon."

"No," PJ said. "Just someone trying to make us think it is. Using all kinds of…well, tricks."

"Ah." Kishan nodded, and thankfully, his smile remained good-natured. "And you think a magician like myself is a prime suspect."

"Not to point fingers, but… Yes," Grant said.

Kishan laughed. "Well, I wish I could say otherwise, but I haven't done as much as a card trick in years. My crate of magic accessories is gathering dust in the attic." He sighed. "Though if the forest would let me in, I might be able to help you peel back the layers of what's going on. If you do think it's a nonmagical causing trouble."

"Do you think we could see that crate?" PJ asked, hoping he wouldn't take the question as an accusation. But it was, unfortunately, the most solid lead they had yet. And if the innkeeper declined, then they'd just have to send Tim up there.

But to his surprise, Kishan nodded. "Sure. But you'll have to brave the dust bunnies upstairs."

"I think we can handle it," Grant said.

They followed Kishan through the kitchen, up the first set of stairs to the second floor, and to the end of the hallway, where a trap door rested with a small pull string that dangled above everyone's heads. Kishan jumped to snag it then pulled the door down, revealing a folded-up ladder and the attic beyond. He made quick work of securing it then climbed up into the darkness, beckoning PJ and Grant to follow him.

"Gosh, now you're making me remember all that I used to do," he said, stooping as he walked through the attic. "I haven't talked about the old life in a long time. Felt like it was a bit dangerous to even pretend to do magic when the queen's people were in and out all the time. I wonder if I should break out some of the old stuff during the busy months, just to drum up some excitement."

"You could add it to your sign at the

crossroads," Grant said. "Magician and delicious custards ahead. And, uh, you should probably consider repainting that sign, too. It's looking a little old."

"That's not a bad idea," Kishan said with a smile as he looked around. "Now, where did I put that crate? I confess, it's been a few years since I've even been up here."

"You said you spent a lot of time at the manor, right?" PJ asked. "Meeting the folks who came and went?"

"Mm." Kishan pulled up a blanket and shook his head. "Yeah, why?"

"Did you ever meet a man named Andres Rade?" PJ asked.

Kishan turned to him, the surprise etched on his face visible even in the scant light. "Andres Rade? What about him? He was a bigwig in the king's service."

"He's coming to visit Ellison soon," PJ said, chancing that this news wouldn't get back to Ellison. "To check out what's going on in the forest."

"Interesting that Ellison's reaching out to folks like that. More interesting that he survived the queen's reign, in my estimation," the innkeeper murmured. "Yeah, he was one of the regulars at Thornhill. Came with some powerful wizards, too.

Four of 'em, I think they protected the king or something. They, in particular, were very interested in my abilities. They swore up and down that I had to have magic as well as I fooled them, but as part of my schtick, I'd wave around an iron skillet from the kitchens." He chuckled. "Wonder what happened to that quartet? Maybe I'll ask Andres about it. When's he coming to town?"

"Soon, I think. But Ellison's not going to have anything to show him if we can't figure out what's going on with the forest," PJ said.

"I can't imagine who'd want to bother the magical folks in there," Kishan said, pulling up another blanket and shaking his head. "Nobody even knows they're in there, except for us. You don't think the forest might be trying to send a message?"

"We've considered that, for sure," PJ said.

"Look, if you want my *honest* opinion," Kishan said, bending over to push some crates out of the way. "I think the forest is tired of having all those people inside it. From what Harold tells me, you couldn't even walk past the tree line if it didn't like you, now it's housing all these people? Probably thought the stragglers would leave, and when they didn't, it took matters into its own hands." He shrugged. "And how are you gonna fight a forest, you know? It's magical. It's sentient. The queen's folks came a few times to try to burn it down, and you see how successful they were. If you've got Ellison's ear, I'd tell him to give up on whatever dream he's got and focus on the here and now, otherwise, the forest is going to do that for him—ah!" He clapped his hands. "Here it is. Right over..." He frowned as he approached a trunk situated against the wall. "Why is it open?"

"What?" PJ asked, walking over to join him. It was difficult to see, but as Kishan knelt before the crate, the front lock had very clearly been tampered with. "Did you leave it unlocked?"

"Never," he said, pulling the lock off and tossing it aside. "Force of habit from traveling. I always lock it. But this..." He opened the trunk and peered in, his mouth falling open as he turned back to PJ and Grant. "I've been robbed."

"Robbed?" PJ repeated, kneeling next to him. "What do you mean?"

"I mean..." He seemed to be taking inventory. "I'm missing my voice-thrower. My disappearing cloak. My sound-keeper." He continued listing things PJ assumed were part of the magician's trade. "They've left my cape and costume, so I don't think they were trying to take my act. But why would they want to take my stuff? It's not like it's worth any money."

"What's a voice-thrower?" PJ asked.

"It's two shells," he said. "You speak into one, and your voice comes out the other end."

"I thought you said you weren't magical," PJ said with narrowing eyes.

Kishan chuckled. "Nonmagical folks are able to use magical things, on occasion. It was my greatest secret, of course. A bevy of tools using the very magic that the wizards and mages had, but they couldn't see the tools." He ran his hand along the empty crate with a sad sigh. "Suppose it's for the best. It's not like I was going to be back out there doing magic tricks anyway."

But PJ looked at the crate, a memory coming to mind of the odd collection he'd found in the forest. "Did you have any vases?"

"Vases?" Kishan nodded. "I suppose my sound-keeper would look like a vase. You could capture a noise or sound in it, then—"

"Then release it later?" PJ finished, looking at Grant. "Venaldra back in Gilramore had something like that, remember? Tim roared into it, and she used that to scare the soldiers off."

Grant nodded, his gaze turning to Kishan. "How loud could it get? Enough to echo through a forest like an ear-splitting roar?"

"The sound-keeper can be amplified," Kishan said. "So you could talk into it, shake it up, then it could be ten times louder than it was."

Those missing pieces were starting to fall into place. Now, at least, they had a *how* and a *why*. They just needed to find the who—and hopefully, the forest would help them with that later this evening.

"I know it's probably a long shot, but do you think you can get my stuff back?" Kishan asked. "Not that it's worth anything but sentimental value…"

PJ made a face. "Depends if the forest is being nice to me or not. I found it when I was wandering in the dark, and it let me stumble upon it. But I haven't a clue how to get back there."

"Don't hurt yourself over it," he said with an understanding nod. "But what I don't understand is…why? Who'd want to scare the handful of magical folks out of the forest?"

"Someone trying to ruin Ellison's plans," Grant said.

"What, you mean selling his house?" Ellison asked.

"That's only if his initial plan doesn't go through," PJ said, looking at Grant for confirmation that they should reveal what Ellison had told them. "He's turning the enclave into a holiday town."

"Holiday…" Kishan blinked, looking as perplexed as PJ had been when Ellison had explained his plans. "What in the world?"

Grant did the honors of explaining the concept, which Kishan, too, thought was an outrageous idea. "He's got that mansion. Why doesn't he just put people up in his house instead?"

"He thinks the forest and the magical folks who live there will be the draw," PJ said. "And he was nearly ready to let the folks in the forest know—"

"They don't know?" Kishan chuckled. "Oh, sweet, stupid Ellison. You special creature."

"I don't think it's a coincidence the nighttime terrors started around the time he was nearing completion of his little project," PJ said. "Nobody in Cheshireville knows about Ellison's plans, do they?"

"No, because if they did, they'd be scrubbing this town until it sparkled." He chuckled. "A whole new crop of customers coming through here? They'd forget all about their dislike of Ellison—and probably agree to help out, too. Laundry, butcher, baker, cidery—it practically blends together."

"I don't think Ellison wants the Cheshireville folks involved," Grant said. "And the way he sounded, they'd be mad about the influx of magical folks."

"They certainly treated us poorly after they found out we were working with Ellison," PJ said.

Kishan shook his head. "They're angry with anyone associated with Ellison, but just having magic? No."

"Ellison said they were cozy with the queen's soldiers," Grant said.

"They were cozy with anyone who gave them coins, because Ellison surely wasn't coughing any up for them," Kishan said. "And sure, they were a *little* surprised when magical creatures poured out of the forest one day. They're good people, don't get me wrong, just not used to seeing purple-haired witches and the like. But if a non-Ellison-affiliated wizard showed up at Adonna's bakery to buy a custard, I doubt she'd turn her nose up at the gold. They make so little of it as it is—and they aren't too happy to hear Ellison's been spending all his coins feeding the strangers in the forest." He shook his head. "Left a bad taste in their mouths. Especially since he's still effectively ignoring them in favor of the forest people, even though they're free to leave and make their own way now."

"Do you think Ellison's holiday plans will be any competition to your business?" Grant asked.

"I mean, he'd have to be successful at it first," Kishan said. "But no. More customers means more money." He looked down at the empty crate again. "But someone very clearly wants Ellison to fail if they're going to all this trouble."

"Who knew you had all this up here?" Grant asked Kishan. "And who has access to the inn's attic?"

"I mean..." He gave a nervous smile. "Everybody in town. I'm not really up on this level except to get the laundry, so if someone wanted to head up here, I might not notice." He stopped, thinking for a moment. "But you know…now that I think about it, Harold was up here a few weeks ago."

"Really?" PJ frowned. "Why?"

"He gave me some story about needing to retrieve something left here by the old owner of the inn," Kishan said. "Seemed weird to me, but I didn't have anything to hide, so I let him. But I wonder if…"

PJ nodded. "I guess we're headed back to Thornhill Manor to ask him about it. Thanks, Kishan. We'll do our best to get your property back."

~

"Ugh, I don't want to have to talk to Harold again," Grant said. "And c'mon, the grumpy, ornery gardener? That seems…I don't know. Way too obvious."

"Obvious or not, it's our next lead," PJ said. "He had access to Kishan's magic tricks, he can come and go in the forest, and he hates the magical folks—and perhaps hates Ellison more." He gave Grant a pointed look. "And I think he might know about Ellison's plans, too. The conversation Tim overheard certainly makes me think he does."

Grant sighed. "Yes, but does that mean we have

to *talk* to him?"

"We should at least give him the opportunity to come clean about it," PJ said as Grant pushed open the iron gate once more and they passed through. "Do you think Ellison's still in the library?"

"You don't want him to see us?" Grant asked.

"Not until we've got some answers," PJ said. "We've been burned a few times by pointing fingers prematurely, and I'd like to avoid that if at all possible."

They didn't have to travel far before they were accosted by Harold, who seemed to have an innate sense for when someone was trespassing on his land. He all but jumped out of the bushes, his trusty rake pointed at PJ and Grant like a weapon.

"What do you two idiots want?" Harold snapped. "If you're looking for Ellison, he's probably at the house. Or with those magical squatters. Or somewhere else. I don't keep up with him."

"We actually wanted to talk to you," PJ said, holding up his hands in surrender. "If you've got a minute."

"I don't." He glowered. "Now get off the property before I—"

"Before you what? We're Ellison's guests," PJ said, though that wasn't strictly true at the present moment. "We're allowed to be here."

He grumbled then skulked away, using his rake as a veritable walking stick. PJ and Grant waited a breath, then PJ followed, with Grant whining behind him about ornery old men and their terrifying gardening equipment.

They followed Harold to a small, glass greenhouse on the corner of the property. The door was open, so PJ walked inside. Harold, aware that he'd been followed, settled gingerly on an old, weathered stool and pulled an empty pot toward him, a collection of herbs sitting beside him, ready to be transplanted.

PJ waited for Harold to speak, but finally decided he'd have to break the ice. "You know, there's a dryad in the forest—"

"I don't care what's in that forest," Harold barked, not turning around. "Don't care if there's a wizard or a mage or a giant bird that's going to flap its wings and knock over all the trees. Don't think it's right for those magical folks to be in there."

"Why not?" PJ asked gently.

"Bah." He turned back to his plants and grew quiet, the only sound coming from him slicing through a stem as he pruned the flowers.

PJ looked at Grant, who shrugged and thumbed for them to leave. But PJ wasn't ready. "We'd like to talk to you about—"

"I ain't talking to you about nothing," he said.

"And if you don't leave, I'm gonna take this shovel and cut off your friend's pretty long tresses." He turned, casting his grizzled gaze on Grant. "His hair's too long anyway. Looks like a ruffian."

"My hair is fine, thank you very much," Grant said, running a hand through it nervously. "And you're mean. You haven't said a nice word to us since we arrived, and we've done nothing to you—"

"You're on my property," he snapped.

"It's Ellison's property, actually," PJ corrected lightly.

"Ellison may be on the title, but he's not the one who's out here, sweating every day to keep it fed and maintained," he growled, rising off his chair. "And he can try to fire me again, but I ain't leaving. He'll have to call his fancy friends at the king's court to come arrest me first!"

"Did you know he'd written to them?" PJ asked, hoping to find some kind of clue that would pin Harold as the culprit.

Harold made a noise as he sat back down. "I don't give a rosebud what he does or doesn't do. All I know is he'd better not try to keep me from this garden. I spent too much of my life here, and I'm not going to leave any time soon. Now I ain't answering any more of your questions—"

"What were you doing in Kishan's attic?" PJ asked.

Harold snorted, digging into the pot of dirt with intensity and ignoring them.

"Are you the one scaring people out of Forest Den?"

No response.

"Looks like he's not talking," Grant said, gesturing toward the door. "Should we? We probably need to meet Ellison soon."

PJ nodded and gestured for Grant to follow him. But once outside, PJ walked quickly toward a hiding spot near the greenhouse, crouching and peering at the building.

"So…what are we doing?" Grant asked.

"I want to see where he goes," PJ said. "And we've got hours until we need to meet Ellison."

Grant studied the sky. "Are you sure about that?"

"Harold's hiding something, and he's not going to tell us about it," PJ said. "So our best bet is to keep an eye on him until he leaves."

"How long are we going to have to sit here?" Grant whined. "I'm hungry. I'm sure the Forest Den folks have already put out the dinner spread. Or Kishan at the inn."

"You could go back to the inn," PJ said. "But I'm staying here. I don't want to miss—"

There was movement in the greenhouse as Harold grabbed a weatherworn coat from a hook near the door and shuffled it on. He padded out slowly, making sure to lock the door behind him. He cast a nervous gaze around, as if he knew he was being watched, then seemed to dismiss the feeling with a loud, "Bah!" He moved as if his joints hurt, easing up the dirt pathway.

PJ slowly emerged from his hiding spot, keeping to the bushes that lined the path. But up ahead, the iron fence that surrounded the property loomed— and the less ornate back gate that was Harold's exit. It opened with a loud *groan* that made the hair on PJ's neck rise then closed just as loudly.

"We're not going to be able to get through that without him hearing us," PJ said.

"I mean, it's not as if he's going very fast," Grant said, gesturing toward him. "We could probably go out the front gate and catch up to him before he made it ten steps down the road."

"Okay, I'll stay here and watch him, and you go around," PJ said, a little exasperatedly. "And if he deviates, I'll tell you which way he went."

"Fine." Grant rose and stretched. "I'm sure he's headed straight for the inn to get dinner. Which is where we should be going, too."

But no sooner had Grant disappeared through the gardens than Harold took a left turn away from the village and toward the forest—and he'd definitely upped his pace. PJ inched closer to the iron bars, looking around for Grant, and cursing when he didn't see him. He touched the iron and winced when it burned his hand.

I help. Tim's voice echoed in PJ's head. *You let go.*

PJ had assumed Tim was going to take over his mind and mentally hover above Harold, but he let out a yelp of surprise when *PJ* took flight. It felt like a gust of wind had swooped in from above, picked him up, and deposited him on the other side.

PJ lay on the grass, blinking at the green blades and wondering what other tricks Tim was hiding up his sleeve. If he hadn't been so shocked, he might've sworn he heard his dragon chuckling at him. But Harold was already moving fast, and PJ didn't have time to waste.

He hopped to his feet and jogged after the gardener, keeping his distance. Not that it would matter, as Harold could just turn around. Grant was still nowhere to be found—perhaps he'd been waylaid by Ellison or gotten lost in the gardens—so PJ was on his own.

"You can't be going into the forest," PJ muttered, but that was exactly what was happening.

As far as PJ could tell, the gardener would only go on behalf of Ellison, and Ellison had clearly stated Harold wasn't doing any more trips today.

But that idea was tested as Harold didn't teeter

toward the forest; rather, he walked along the edge of the tree line. PJ needed a hiding spot—not exactly easy in the open field. He dashed toward the forest, hoping he could keep out of sight while not straying too far inside. Once the shadows were overhead, that familiar pressure on his magic returned. Though the forest didn't kick him out, exactly, PJ was well aware that he was only being offered limited access.

PJ was still able to talk with Tim, who would dash ahead to check on the gardener and look for anything suspicious.

He just walk.

"Where is he going?" PJ asked.

All woods. I see nothing.

The sun moved closer to the horizon, and PJ considered whether he should turn around. But Harold was clearly going somewhere.

"Maybe his house is all the way up here," PJ muttered.

But up ahead, the forest curved around to cover the field, and PJ saw nothing but trees. Harold walked perpendicular to the tree line as if he intended to enter until he stopped.

Then PJ's magical senses tingled as the forest shuddered then split. And to PJ's absolute shock, the massive typhon emerged from the trees. In the broad daylight, the image was strikingly similar to the line drawing in the encyclopedia. It had a pale face with dark spots on his bald head. The long nose and large ears reminded PJ of his old neighbor back in Pigsend, and the smile on the typhon's face was almost endearing.

With effort, the typhon knelt in front of Harold, who pulled something out of his bag and waved it around. The giant placed his massive hand on the ground, palm up, and Harold carefully climbed up and sat. Then the typhon rose, with Harold in hand, and turned to venture back into the forest.

PJ sprinted toward the typhon as fast as his human legs could carry him. But as soon as he reached the forest, something grabbed him by the arms and flung him backward. He tumbled, head over feet, until landing with a loud *oof* on the ground, staring up at the sky.

It took PJ a minute to realize what had happened. Stars danced in front of his eyes as he came back to himself, and he blinked them away as he sat up. He moved all his extremities to make sure they still worked then rubbed his face roughly to clear the fog from his mind.

"Well, if that wasn't the most incriminating thing," PJ said.

Maybe, came Tim's reply. *Typhon not near village, remember?*

"Right, but…" PJ was grasping at threads again. "Okay, so we have Harold, who was up in Kishan's attic recently. Harold, who hates the magical folks in the village, but clearly not the forest itself. Harold, who has not only seen the typhon, but apparently, is friendly enough to be carried by him." PJ ticked off his fingers. "That's a lot pointing to him as the culprit. Even if the typhon was nowhere near the village, it doesn't mean Harold still isn't behind it himself."

Tim let out a snort of agreement. *Learn more first.*

"I was planning on it," PJ said. "I learned my lesson back in Padstow."

As he wasn't going to be following the creature anymore, PJ gingerly got to his feet and began the long trek back toward Cheshireville. Without having to hide from the slow-moving gardener, PJ was back in town within twenty minutes. He assumed Grant wasn't still at Ellison's house, so he headed straight for the inn.

It was dinnertime, and everyone from town had come to the inn in search of a meal. Roe and Oscar weren't there, of course, but Adonna, Brennan, Ulysses, and Orlena were all seated around their usual table. Grant had joined them as well, rising immediately when PJ walked in.

"Has Ellison come by yet?" PJ asked.

"Not yet," Grant said. "Where'd you go?"

"I've got to talk to you about some stuff," PJ

said, gesturing for him to follow. He obviously wasn't going to talk about the typhon and Harold in front of the townsfolk.

"Can't we do it after dinner?" Grant whined. "I hear it's roast beef tonight."

"I'd like to get a plan together before Ellison comes back," PJ said, keeping his voice low. "Because—"

"It's no use hiding," Adonna said flatly. "We know about his plans."

The others at the table nodded, and PJ scowled at Grant. "You told them?"

"I didn't!" Grant held up his hands in surrender. "I swear!"

"I told them," Kishan said, walking out of the kitchen. "I don't understand why it's such a big secret anyway. If Ellison's going to be bringing new people to town, the folks here ought to know about it ahead of time so they can decide if they want to stay or go."

"You say Ellison's coming here to escort you into the forest?" Adonna asked. "We'd like to ask him about this."

"And let us come into the forest as well," Ulysses said. "After all, why shouldn't we have access to all these new people?"

"W-what are you all talking about?" Ellison asked, walking into the inn with a bewildered look on his face. "Erm, PJ? Grant?"

"We know about your holiday town plans," Orlena said, giving him a sideways look. "When were you going to inform *us* about it?"

Ellison's face flushed. "As soon as they were confirmed. But they're not, so..." He laughed nervously, his gaze sweeping to PJ and Grant. "You told them?"

"It doesn't matter how we found out," Brennan said. "We want in."

"Yeah," Adonna said. "You can't cut us out of this deal, Ellison. If you're going to be drawing people to that village, you need to hire us to help."

"The thing is... Erm, as a matter of fact..." Ellison stammered, his face roughly the color of a tomato. "We're not even remotely close to..."

"Ellison's not ready to share the details yet," PJ said, hoping to save the poor man from the wrath of his fellow townsfolk. "In fact, he was ready to share it, then someone decided to cause trouble for the enclave, thus scaring most of the folks away. And we think the culprit might be right here in this room."

The townsfolk looked at each other, their anger evaporating at the accusation. "None of us have even been able to set *foot* in the forest," Ulysses said.

"It tossed us out," Orlena replied. "Which, you'd better *fix* before you start inviting people, Ellison."

"I, erm, plan on it," Ellison muttered, inching toward the door. "But the sun's starting to set, and we do have to load up more supplies for the town, so—"

"Supplies you paid for?" Brennan asked with a glare. "Instead of spending your money here in the village? Instead of supporting *us*, the people who used to work for your father?"

"Magic's legal again," Adonna said, throwing her hands in the air. "Why don't those people make their own way like the rest of us? What's so special about them that you keep giving them money?"

"Ellison's right," Grant said, stepping between the angry crowd and the red-faced merchant's son. "We've got to get a move on. We'll be sure to have a full discussion with you fine folks in the morning about Ellison's plans, and how you fit into them. Because I'm *quite sure* he's got plans for you." He turned to Ellison. "Don't you?"

Ellison seemed to have swallowed his tongue and his ability to speak.

"He does," PJ said. "Kishan? Where would we find those supplies?"

"Round the back," the innkeeper said, thumbing toward the kitchen. "Just be mindful you don't mess up anything back there again. Took me hours to fix what Harold broke the other day."

"Will do," Grant said, flashing him and

everyone else a smile before shoving Ellison through the door.

"Well, this is a disaster," Ellison said with a sigh as they led the wagon and horse to the back of the inn. A small collection of crates sat just beyond the back door, ready to be loaded.

"How so?" PJ asked, picking up the first crate and placing it on the back of the wagon. "They all seem like they're ready to be on board with it."

"Because the whole point of a magical town is to have *magical* people in it," Ellison said with a furtive look back. "You can find a cider maker or a launderer in any old town. The draw to Forest Den is that it's full of magical folks." He sighed. "Well, it was... Hopefully, I can invite more magical people back. Once we're up and running."

"Or, you could have a mix of folks," Grant said, quirking an eyebrow as he added another crate to the wagon. "Even if Orlena travels there to pick up the bedsheets and brings them back to clean, or Brennan drops off his casks, the people are still going to be visiting an enchanted forest."

Ellison shifted. "I'm not sure... I mean... You really shouldn't have told anyone. I trusted you not to."

"We told Kishan," PJ said, thumbing toward the back door. "He told the rest of the town. But he also told us something interesting: Harold was in his attic."

"I don't see why I should care about that," Ellison said. "Harold's allowed to go wherever he wants, you know."

"Yes, but Kishan's magic tricks were stolen," Grant said. "And PJ thinks he saw those magic tricks in the forest the other day."

Ellison still seemed not to understand.

"Someone's using Kishan's stolen magic tricks to make it seem like the typhon is terrorizing the town," PJ said plainly.

Realization dawned on the young man. "Oh. To sabotage me, right?"

PJ and Grant nodded.

"Oh, goodness. Well, that's... How long has Kishan known his things have been burgled?"

"He said he rarely goes up to the attic, but he took us up there today, and that's when he discovered his trunk had been broken into," PJ said. "And there's more. I followed Harold from the house to the forest. He walked a ways out of town, and then..." He considered his phrasing. Just the facts. "Then I saw the typhon walk out of the forest, scoop him up, and take him inside."

"Goodness!" Ellison almost dropped the crate. "We have to save him!"

"He wasn't in distress," PJ said. "He seems to be

friends with the typhon."

Ellison worked his jaw, and Grant tilted his head at PJ. "You don't seem to think this is the incriminating evidence we were looking for, do you?"

"I'd like to ask him about it before we go accusing him of something."

"We tried that earlier," Grant said.

"Then we'll try again. I'm not sure he can refuse to answer my questions if I tell him I saw him with the thing that's supposedly terrorizing the village," PJ said, picking up the last crate. "But as it stands, we're not going to be able to talk to him tonight. And I'd much rather be in the village when and if our culprit tries again."

"Or we can tell Harold to nicely ask the typhon to leave the village alone," Ellison said.

PJ opened his mouth to argue but instead just shook his head. "While we're on the subject of Forest Den, you should tell them about your plans, too. It's only fair, Ellison."

"Agreed," Grant said. "You're turning their homes into a theater show. They deserve to know about it and have a say in whether or not you go through with it."

"But what if they say no?" Ellison asked softly. "I've spent every gold coin I have keeping them fed and happy. I don't know what I'll do if…"

"Talk to them," PJ said, after a moment. "You don't have to keep everything so close to the vest, you know. The people in Forest Den really appreciate all you've done for them. They might not be too upset by the idea, you know? But it seems to me you've been making decisions for people all this time without really asking what they think. And that's usually a recipe for disaster."

Ellison nodded. "None of this is going to matter if there's no one left in the forest, though."

"Leave that to us," PJ said. "I have a feeling we're going to get close to finding our culprit tonight."

If the forest cooperated.

~

At first blush, the forest seemed to be in a good mood. The trees on the edge picked themselves up by their roots and walked out of the way of the wagon. But as soon as PJ fell under the shadow of the first tree, that all-encompassing pressure on his chest resumed as well, and Tim was no longer palpable in his mind. This time, PJ had expected it and was feeling quite ready to face whatever met them this evening.

"Tim gone again?" Grant asked.

PJ nodded, rubbing his chest. "I'm okay with it. We'll see what tonight brings."

"What are you talking about?" Ellison asked.

"Nothing," PJ said, not wanting to worry him.

They found the small collection of tree houses within a few minutes, and the sight of the wagon drew the villagers from their houses, the magical creatures crowding around to retrieve the supplies they'd ordered.

"Right-o," Pat said, finding his potatoes by sniffing the crates. "Too late for the potluck, but I can make some delicious taters tomorrow."

"You're back, eh?" Hilde said to PJ and Grant. "Figure out what kinda monster we're contending with?"

"We actually have some, erm, news about all that," Ellison said, his face resuming its red color. "Has the potluck started yet?"

"Just about," Bill said, thumbing toward the mushrooms where the food was spread out. "Just missing a few people."

"G-good," Ellison said, dismounting the wagon. "Because I've got an announcement to make, and I want everyone here."

It didn't take long. The stragglers, Audra and Ingrid, arrived with their dishes moments after Ellison sat on one of the mushrooms, fidgeting. PJ and Grant stood off to the side, as Ellison needed to make this announcement by himself.

"Well?" Bill asked, after Audra sat next to her wife. "What's the big news, Ellison?"

"I think it's time that you folks hear what I've been up to," he said, nervously. "Erm, as you know, I've been, erm, doing some things with Bill in the vacant houses, and, erm—"

"Out with it," Hilde barked.

"I'd like to turn Forest Den into a tourist town," Ellison said, his gaze still plastered on the ground. "Invite magical and nonmagical folks to come stay in the vacant houses. Enjoy the community we've built here. I think it might be…" He seemed to take in the surprise on everyone's faces. "That is, if you folks would allow it."

"You mean, if the *forest* would allow it," Hilde said with a scoff. "You've got to be joking, Ellison."

"I think it could work," Pat said, his tail wagging. "I mean, I got a brother who said he'd love to visit me here. Wouldn't it be fine if I had a place for him to stay?"

"What's involved in this holiday town?" Audra asked, glancing at her wife. "And what would we be expected to do?"

"I'd handle all the administrative stuff," Ellison said, quickly. "Have the folks pay a small fee for their room and board, and divvy it up amongst us, you know? Bill, you could sell your woodworking, and Hilde, you could sell your baskets, too."

"And what if we don't want to have strangers in our town?" Hilde asked, with a raised brow.

"Then you're gonna have to leave," Grant said, crossing his arms. "Because Ellison's out of money to pay for your potatoes and flowers and whatever else you're having him buy. The queen is gone, and you folks are gonna have to make your own way in the big world. And I think you'll be hard-pressed to find travelers who'll come all the way into this forest without something to look forward to."

Surprise rippled across the faces of those in the crowd. Ellison looked at his hands, but he didn't contradict Grant. PJ waited for the first person to argue, to say they were ready to leave, but no one did. Perhaps Ellison had been right to assume they'd want to follow his crazy plan.

"Don't think of it like a holiday spot," PJ said, after a moment. "Think of it as a way to attract customers far off the beaten path. We've been out and about on the main road, and Cheshireville is easy to miss. The innkeeper in the village beyond had to put a sign at the fork in the road. That's the only reason we even knew their village existed."

"Well, nobody's coming to Forest Den if we don't get this monster to leave us alone," Delaney said, turning to PJ and Grant. "You two have been gone all day. Surely, you've got an answer, don't you?"

"We're getting close to one," PJ said with a nod. "I—"

A loud, pained moan echoed from the forest beyond, causing the hairs on PJ's arms to stand up. *"Getttt...ouuuuuuut."*

"Okay, that's new," Grant said with a nervous swallow. "Haven't heard anyone talk before."

A loud *thump...thump...thump...* reverberated in PJ's chest. The movement was slow, sounding more like a heavy weight dragging through the forest. Very close to the typhon.

"Look!" Hilde pointed at the forest beyond. There, in the mist illuminated by the faint light of the night sky, was a shadow as tall as the trees, with thick arms and legs, carrying what appeared to be a massive club.

"Getttt...ouuuuuuuuuuuut!" the voice bellowed again.

"W-what is that?" Ellison said, his eyes wild. "This can't be the same creature."

"Yes," PJ said with a frown. Once again, there was no sense of danger, no typhon nearby. "This is new."

"Leeeeeeave! Oooor elllllllsssse!"

"Nice try," Grant called to the forest. "But we know you're not real. Now show yourself so—"

Crack.

"What was that?" PJ said, tilting his head toward the canopy overhead.

"Look out!" Ingrid cried. "Everybody scatter!"

PJ grabbed Grant, who was still looking for the culprit in the shadows of the trees, and yanked him away from the tavern moments before a massive tree branch landed in the center of the dining room with a deafening *thud.*

CHAPTER SIXTEEN

"Is everyone okay?" Bill asked as soon as the echoing stopped.

The townsfolk had dispersed quickly, and luckily, the only thing hurt was the delicious dinner that had been waiting to be enjoyed—and the mushrooms that had made up the outdoor tavern. Grant walked up to the broken platters sadly, picking at some of the potatoes that had escaped being crushed.

"What a waste…" He sighed.

PJ walked over to the fallen tree limb and examined it closely. It had definitely broken off, but there was also the telltale sign of sawing. Someone had started cutting it then let gravity do the rest of the work, hoping their sabotage wouldn't be noticed.

The work of a gardener, perhaps?

Bill walked over to inspect the branch. "It's a nice piece of wood. I could probably turn it into some fine furniture." He nodded to the mushrooms crushed underneath it. "Could've done without them ruining dinner and our tavern, though."

"I really liked those mushrooms, too," Ellison said with a sigh. "It was going to be part of the charm. Do you think we can fix them, Ingrid?"

"Mushrooms are pretty hardy," she said with a kind pat on his shoulder. "But the Pearlwinds were the ones who put them up in the first place. Perhaps they'll be willing to stop in for a visit and rebuild them."

"Assuming no more branches fall," Bill said, gazing warily at the canopy above. "I'll get to work on clearing the branch now. Let me get my axe."

The centaur turned to walk back toward his home, leaving Ingrid, Ellison, Grant, and PJ to assess the damage. Ellison whimpered about the ambiance of the village while Ingrid hopped over the fallen branch in a vain attempt to salvage anything that had been on the potluck spread.

"What do you think?" Grant asked, coming to stand next to PJ, who was inspecting the rest of the branch for signs of cuts.

"Someone clearly heard us say the monster isn't dangerous and wanted us to think otherwise," PJ said, keeping his voice low.

"You can't have Tim do a sweep to look for the culprit, can you?" Grant asked, tilting his head up. "You'd think the forest would want us to know who's cutting off limbs."

"It's strange." Ingrid touched the sawed-off part gently. "I just asked several trees what happened, and they couldn't tell me. They said they were… they were told not to."

"By whom?" PJ asked.

She shook her head, her hand coming to her mouth.

"My axe is missing," Bill said, his hooves clopping on the ground as he walked over. He wore a frown as he approached, inspecting the broken limb. "And it looks like it was used to chop this tree down."

"How…?" PJ said. "We would've heard it, right? It's not like someone could whack a tree—"

"We were probably all distracted by the sounds of the monster," Grant said. "I mean, I know I wasn't paying attention to anything but the creepy voice telling me to vacate the premises."

"Whoever is doing this has no qualms about stealing," PJ said. "First Kishan's magical tricks, now

Bill's axe. What's next?"

"I'm not sticking around to find out." Hilde, who'd run to her house, had reappeared carrying what appeared to be everything she owned, wrapped up in a large floral sheet and hooked onto a staff. She'd left her door open, clearly not worrying about coming back. "You all have a lovely time setting up this magical holiday village without me. I'll be at my sister's."

"Wait!" Ellison jogged over. "Hilde, you can't leave. We're so close to—And your basket weaving!"

"I'll weave baskets and sell 'em at my sister's house," Hilde said with a snort. "Look, it was one thing when it was just a creature making a lot of ruckus. I could *mostly* deal with that. But tree branches falling on our heads is where I draw the line, Ellison." She turned on her heel and walked toward the forest. "Have a good life, all of you."

The forest, perhaps sensing that the small and formidable woman wasn't to be trifled with, opened a path for her to walk out, closing back up as soon as her purple hair had passed.

"Oh, goodness, Hilde..." Ingrid said with a sigh.

"She's not wrong," Audra said, holding her middle. "Someone wants to hurt us. They dropped a branch right on our heads. Ellison, I know you've done so much for us..."

"I'm not leaving," Bill said, crossing his arms over his chest. "They can try to scare us out, but that only strengthens my resolve to stay. I've spent too much time making this place my home."

"Hear, hear," Pat said.

"I agree, honey," Delaney said to her wife with a solemn nod. "If someone wants us to leave, they're going to have to try harder than this to do it."

One by one, they turned to Ellison, who was still nervously glancing at the sky. "You all really want to stay that badly?"

"This is our part of the forest," Ingrid said, surprisingly determined. "They'll have to drop all the branches on us. We're not going anywhere."

The townsfolk were keen to stay, but Ellison seemed unnerved by the whole thing, murmuring excuses about needing to get the horse and wagon back to the house before Harold had a conniption. Luckily, the horse had been tied up far enough away from the commotion that it hadn't reacted to the falling branch, but it seemed ready to leave the magical forest as Ellison untied it.

"Well, this has been…an interesting night," Ellison glanced at the trees above. "I can't believe someone really wants to disrupt all this for…for what? Just to get back at me?"

"The better question is why they escalated their

efforts," PJ said, looking at Grant. "I think it's wise for us to stay here tonight. Just in case they try again."

"You don't think they're going to drop any more limbs on the townsfolk, do you?"

"They'd have a hard time doing that with everyone asleep in their beds," PJ said. "But we should see if Ingrid's up for a nighttime jaunt through the forest. I want to look for clues. Maybe even climb a tree and find the sawed-off limb."

"Why are you two so invested in this?" Ellison asked quietly. "You're strangers. I wouldn't blame you if you were gone in the morning."

PJ smiled. "This is our job. We're tasked to help people who need it. And clearly, you guys need it."

Ellison thanked them again then headed back home as fast as the mare would walk—which was quite fast, considering her age. PJ and Grant lingered, assessing the town as the folks said their goodnights to each other, while keeping wary of the canopy above.

"So what's our plan tonight?" Grant asked. "Another romp through the forest? Climbing up to the treetops to look for Bill's axe? Or are we going to hunt down the typhon and ask it why it's got a problem with Forest Den?"

"The typhon wasn't here," PJ said. "Our culprit was using Kishan's magic tricks to do all that. I'm sure of it."

"They didn't use the tricks to cut down the limb," Grant said with a frown. "That really happened." He glanced at the treetops. "I wonder how he got up there?"

"Only one way to find out," PJ said with a mischievous grin. "Time to climb."

"Oh, no," Grant said, holding up his hands. "I'm not breaking my neck—and you shouldn't, either. Not when you don't have Tim around to—"

I here.

PJ's eyes bulged. "Tim?"

"He's back?" Grant asked.

Forest keep contained. But now let speak.

"Can you look around for trouble?" PJ asked, breathless. "Maybe scan the surrounding areas? Do you think the forest would—"

I contained.

PJ stopped, frowning. "So you can talk to me, but that's about it, eh? That's…an improvement, I guess."

You climb tree. I help. Grant stay ground.

"Tim says you should stay here," PJ said, nervous energy skittering in his chest. Tim had been able to launch PJ over the fence earlier, but that was without any constraints. He could talk now, but how much more could he do?

"Are you sure about this?" Grant asked. "It's

pretty high."

"I trust Tim's judgment," PJ said weakly. "You stay here and keep an eye on things."

Tim pointed him toward one of the houses that appeared knobbier than the rest, with twists and turns in the trunk instead of a smooth bark. PJ ensured the house was vacant before clambering up the protruding parts. He wasn't sure if the tree was assisting him, or if his limited dragon senses were finally working, but he kept moving as long as he had spots for his hands and feet. After a while, he sensed he was getting pretty high up on the tree, though he didn't dare look down.

You no fall.

"Thanks, Tim," PJ said.

Finally, he was close enough to pull himself up onto a branch, settling himself firmly on it before hazarding a glance at the town below. The branch was at least five stories high, and although that fact alone made his head swim, he could still go higher.

"What do you see, Tim?" PJ asked.

Look up. Path.

PJ hadn't noticed it on the climb up, but his mouth fell open when he spotted it.

A wooden bridge, suspended above the town with rope.

PJ stood and braced himself against the trunk, just until he could slip his fingers over the edge of the wooden planks. He pulled himself up with a silent prayer that it wouldn't break under his weight. Despite its apparent age, it seemed rather sturdy.

"Okay," PJ said, finding his balance with the rope handrails that ran on either side. "Let's see where this goes…"

He walked slowly, being sure to test each plank before putting his full weight on it, until he spotted where the branch had been sawed off—and Bill's axe resting against the trunk.

"Did Harold cut down this tree limb?" PJ asked the trees surrounding him.

The forest shook as if a breeze had just blown past.

"You're not gonna tell me, hm?" PJ said. "Why are you protecting whoever's doing it? Do you want everyone to leave?"

Forest confused.

"You can talk to the forest?" PJ asked Tim.

Forest speak in natural language. I understand basic.

"Then tell me why it's confused," PJ said.

Forest like people. Forest want people stay. Forest not know why no can tell.

PJ couldn't really make sense of that. "What about the typhon?"

Typhon no harm town. Typhon too far.

He looked at the axe. "What about Kishan's magic tricks? Does the forest want to give those up?"

Forest not know where is. Moved.

PJ clicked his tongue. "Question for you, Tim. What could be confusing the forest?"

Magic of some kind. I sense disturbance but not know where.

"Disturbance?" PJ recalled what Ingrid had said. "I wonder if that's what Ingrid was talking about, too."

I look.

Tim took over PJ's eyes, the familiar burning sensation welcome after a long absence, but unlike outside the forest, where Tim's range of vision was long, here he couldn't go farther than PJ's body. But even with limited sight, PJ took advantage of having his dragon senses. The village below was now brightly lit, surrounded by misty magic that permeated every inch of the forest, with larger concentrations inside the non-vacant homes. Beyond the village, the magic was much more pronounced, but for once, PJ wasn't afraid of what it might bring.

"Shall we see where this bridge leads?" PJ said.

Then, grateful for Tim's presence, he turned and began walking down the elevated wooden bridge, girding himself for whatever he might find. The farther he went from the village, the more he heard the telltale sounds of owls, foxes, and maybe even the howl of a wolf. PJ stopped intermittently to look down but saw nothing of interest. That was, until he passed the footprint they'd found the other day. It was still there, though with the assistance of Tim's vision, he could see that there was now a large puddle of magic in the ground just beneath the surface.

He leaned down, narrowing his gaze. "That's a lot of magic concentrated there, isn't it?"

Agree.

"Do you think it's a natural source?" PJ asked. "Like the wellspring in Padstow?"

Don't tell gnome.

PJ stood upright, a smile blossoming on his face. "Tim, was that a joke?"

I funny sometime. Learn from human.

"I'll have to tell Grant he's got competition for the funniest person in the group," PJ said, focusing on the footprint again. Something about it drew his attention, but he wasn't sure if he was just overthinking things. From the looks of it, it appeared to be a normal pool of magic, like a pond he'd seen in the forests of Gilramore, and there was nothing more interesting about it than that.

PJ kept on the path, even though the forest below was looking darker and wilder. This *had* to be leading somewhere. Finally, after he was sure that someone had built an entire wooden bridge to nowhere, Tim spoke again.

Up ahead.

"Is that a house?"

PJ approached quietly, just in case there was someone there. The hairs on his arms rose, signaling the nearness of the typhon. He looked this way and that, but even with Tim's eyes, he couldn't see it yet.

The house had no doors or windows and looked more like a playhouse for children. PJ cautiously peered inside, exhaling when he found the single room vacant. There wasn't a bed, nor chairs, nor curtains, but there was a chest in the corner, old, weathered teddy bears, and lots of spiderwebs. He did spy a collection of children's books, all of which had a greenish tint from being outside for too long.

SNOOOOORE.

PJ jumped so high he almost fell out of the tree house. He clutched his chest, spinning around to find the source of the noise. Tim took over, giving the darkness a closer look, and he, too, found nothing.

SNOOOOORE.

PJ crept to the window, heart pounding, and gazed down from the tree house. There, in a large valley, sleeping quite peacefully, was the typhon.

CHAPTER SEVENTEEN

PJ was afraid to move, fearing if he did, the monster would wake up and throw him from the house. But after a few minutes, he finally relaxed, processing what was in front of him instead of being gutted by it.

The typhon had either cleared out a valley, or perhaps, over the years, the sheer weight of it had caused an indent in the rocky forest floor. The trees had clearly moved out of his way, lest they be crushed, leaving nothing but boulders and rocky outcroppings in the valley below. The typhon's massive head was resting on one such outcropping, which PJ had to assume wasn't very comfortable at all.

Still, he wasn't keen to stick around and see if the discomfort would rouse the giant, so as quietly as humanly possible, he inched backward through the tree house, leaving the teddy bears and books behind, and started back on the wooden walkway toward the village. He moved much faster than before, both because he knew where to step and also because he felt *safer* the farther he got from the typhon.

In fact, he wasn't sure he took a deep breath until he was right above the village, snagging Bill's axe from where he'd left it and starting the climb down—which was a little more hazardous with an axe to handle.

I help.

Tim unlocked PJ's fingers from the tree and he fell backward, letting out a cry of surprise. But as with the gate, a gust of air surrounded PJ and he floated gently to the ground. He collapsed to his knees, exhaling loudly as he clutched the sandy ground beneath his fingertips.

"Tim, that wasn't... *Don't do that again*," PJ spat.

You fine.

"Who are you talking to?" Ingrid stood before him, tilting her head in confusion.

PJ pushed himself up and shook his head. "No one. Sorry. Didn't mean to wake you up."

"I couldn't sleep," she said before her eyebrows rose. "Where'd you find Bill's axe?"

"Up in the trees," PJ said. "Did you know there's a whole walkway up there?"

Based on Ingrid's confused expression, she'd had no idea. "What are you talking about?"

PJ left Bill's axe on his front step, and Ingrid became more and more perplexed as PJ told her about the bridge, the tree house, and the typhon sleeping at the end of it.

"I can't believe I didn't know about any of that," Ingrid said with a sigh. "I thought the forest and I were honest with each other. It was always so kind, answering my questions, working with us as we moved here. I never once felt threatened or..." She tilted her head up toward the canopy.

"My, erm, dragon says the forest is confused," PJ said. "Like it wants to do one thing, but it's being coerced to do another. I don't know who'd have the power to do all that, though. Certainly not anyone in this forest. No one we've come across in the village, either."

"That would explain why it's been so agitated lately," Ingrid said, looking mildly angry—which, for her, was saying something. "But other than me, who'd have the power to commune with plants?"

"Harold, perhaps," PJ said, telling Ingrid about the greenhouse and how loyal Harold had been to

Ellison's plants. "I saw him yesterday with the typhon, too."

Ingrid frowned. "You didn't think to mention that to us?"

"I'm not sure how it all fits together, to be honest," PJ said. "Yes, he's ornery. Yes, he's got a vendetta against Forest Den. Yes, he hates Ellison. But…" PJ pointed toward the canopy. "Even if the typhon put him up in the tree house, that's a long way to walk with that heavy axe. And even cutting the limb down seems too much for an old man to handle." He looked around the village. "But at the same time, he's very friendly with the forest. I tried to follow him and it threw me out."

"What will you do next?" Ingrid asked.

"Find Harold," PJ said. "Try to squeeze the truth out of him. May have to call on my dragon to scare it out of him, at this point. But if he's got a typhon for a friend, he probably doesn't scare easily." He turned to Ingrid. "You know, the two of you would probably get along. He really loves plants. I wish we could figure out why he's so dead set against you folks. Maybe we could convince him it's not so bad."

Ingrid smiled. "You've got a kind heart, PJ. Even through all this discontent, you're still looking for the good in Harold. I think that's a very rare, very wonderful quality. And I'm sure it's served you well on your investigations, too."

PJ's face warmed.

~

Thankfully, no more limbs dropped during the night, and when morning came, the townsfolk gathered around what was left of their outdoor dining room with baskets of food and tea as if nothing had happened. It seemed the escalation had only served to embolden them into sticking around, which made PJ happy—and a little concerned. If the culprit was willing to drop a tree limb on the town, what else was he planning to do to get them to leave?

PJ had asked Ingrid not to share what he'd learned about the typhon, the walkway, or Harold until he had more information. The dryad seemed to understand and showed no signs that she knew there was an overhead path.

Grant, however, could not be trusted to react so quietly, so PJ waited until they'd had their fill of breakfast, which included a biscuit sandwich of dried meat and cheese, and Ingrid had escorted them out of the forest before he filled Grant in.

"Are you...*serious*?" Grant gawped at him. "Okay, first of all—you can fly?"

"Jump high and fall gracefully," PJ corrected lightly. "And neither one is a pleasant experience, so let's just skip over that."

"Second, you found Bill's axe and a wooden walkway that led right to the typhon's house?" he continued.

"The house was too small to be the typhon's, and it didn't look like a house someone lived in, either," PJ said, still trying to piece things together in his mind. "But it was right next to where the typhon was sleeping, so not a stretch to think they're connected. I think it's time we confront Harold—really confront him—and get him to come clean about everything."

Finding Harold was easier said than done. The boys were able to walk right onto the Thornhill Manor grounds without any harassment and search the house until they found Ellison in his office.

"Goodness!" Ellison jumped to his feet, clearly not expecting anyone to visit, and only slowly settled back into his chair. "What are you two doing here?"

"We're looking for your gardener," PJ said. "Have you seen him?"

"No, and…honestly, I'm worried," Ellison said, rising to look out his window onto the garden. "He never takes a day off, not even when it's snowing or raining. He's always puttering around here. But I haven't seen him this morning." He turned to the boys. "You said the typhon took him, right? Maybe he's in trouble."

"As I said yesterday, they looked like friends," PJ said. "And I discovered some things last night about the forest."

Like Ingrid, Ellison seemed to have no clue about the walkway, or the tree house, or that they both were connected to the typhon. He was especially interested to hear that Bill's missing axe had been found on the walkway, which also made him incredibly anxious.

"Well, I hope Bill's secured it now," he said, wringing his hands. "What if our culprit comes back? What if he finds another axe? Do you think I should lock up Harold's tools to make sure it doesn't—"

"I think we should focus on finding Harold first," PJ said. "Where does he live, Ellison?"

"Erm." Ellison's face warmed. "I'm actually not sure. Maybe the villagers would know? I don't..." He cleared his throat, clearly uncomfortable. "I don't really track where..."

PJ sighed. "Fine, we'll head to the inn to ask where he lives. Maybe he's taken ill or something."

"Or he's hanging out in the forest," Grant leaned back in the chair. "I got a theory that might explain everything."

"Do share," PJ said dryly.

"So, a thousand years ago, when Harold was a young man," Grant said with a mischievous smirk, "he became friends with the typhon. Probably because he liked hanging out in the forest. He's part dryad, like Ingrid."

"You think he's part dryad?" PJ asked with a quirked brow.

"Maybe distantly dryad, but he's got an affinity for plants," Grant continued, waving PJ off. "So he builds himself a little treetop walkway to get from here to there, high up so he can hang out with his giant friend, and a little house to play in, maybe. Or maybe his dad did, who knows?" Grant shook his head. "In any case, then along comes this crowd of magical folks invading his beloved forest. Now he's worried they're gonna find his giant typhon friend or ruin his forest or whatever."

"But no one knew the typhon was there," Ellison said.

"Harold's not being rational. He's living in fear that these folks are gonna find his giant buddy and do something bad to him," Grant said. "So then, the queen's out of power, and Harold wants his peaceful forest back. Half the town leaves of their own free will, great. But now…now Harold wants the rest of 'em to leave. So he steals Kishan's magic tricks and, with the forest's help, makes it look like his typhon is attacking, but of course, the typhon is safely on the other side of the forest."

PJ nodded slowly. It was making sense, except…

"I don't know if Harold is physically capable of wielding that axe."

"You can do crazy things when you're mad enough about something," Grant said. "Especially if, as he might've found out yesterday, Ellison was planning to bring *even more* people to his quiet little forest. That might've made him eager to ratchet things up, like dropping a limb on the town."

PJ couldn't deny that the theory was solid, and yet, his theories in other towns had also been solid, and he'd been missing a crucial piece of evidence that had revealed the truth.

"We can cast theories all day, but we won't get the real answer until we corner Harold. I think we should split up to look for him," PJ said. "Check the town and the surrounding areas first. Maybe the forest will be more compliant today."

"Don't count on it," Grant muttered.

"And if we don't find him in town, we can maybe head up to the walkway and venture back to the tree house," PJ said, though he didn't even want to consider that as an option. He'd already gotten too close to the typhon as it was, and he didn't want to go any nearer when it was awake. "And keep in mind that Harold might actually be innocent."

"I don't believe that," Ellison said. "Grant builds a good case."

PJ sighed. "Fine. Let's just find him first.

Ellison, you take the town—"

"I'd rather not, if it's okay with you," Ellison said nervously. "After yesterday, I'm not sure the townsfolk are feeling very…" He cleared his throat. "Um, anyway. I'll stick to the grounds and the gardens here, if it's all right with you."

~

"What a coward," Grant muttered as he and PJ left the manor. "'The townsfolk are mad at me, so I don't want to show my face.' Is he just going to hide in his house forever?"

"He's banking on them seeing the parade of magical folks and leaving," PJ said, glancing back. "That's what he told us yesterday."

"See? Coward." Grant sniffed. "Still, it does beg the question: What did they do to Ellison?"

"Hm?"

"I mean, it's one thing for them to hate Ellison —he canned them and stopped paying them," Grant said. "But Ellison's clearly got some bad blood of his own with them. Wonder what that is?"

"I'm sure they'd be *happy* to tell us," PJ said with a snort as they approached Cheshireville. But he stopped, spotting movement in the distance—a group of people were moving rapidly toward the village.

"Soldiers?" Grant said with a frown. "What are soldiers doing here?"

"Queen or kingside?" PJ asked, a drop of fear sliding down his chest.

"King, dummy," Grant said, nudging him. "Queen's out of power."

"I mean, you never know." PJ nudged him back but still exhaled in relief when Tim confirmed the colors they were wearing. "Maybe they're here to answer Ellison's letter."

The duo walked across the field to meet the collection of soldiers. Some were on horseback, others on foot. The horses were magnificent, bearing riders wearing the finest material in the king's colors. Every one had a lethal-looking weapon on them, which reminded PJ of the soldiers who'd come through Pigsend to cause trouble. But while they certainly looked intimidating, they had an ease about them that quieted PJ's nerves.

The leader, an imposing gentleman with a bald head and dark brown skin, who carried himself like a soldier used to leading armies, waved them down as they approached. "Oh, I thought you were someone else," the man said, his voice low and booming and somewhat comforting. "I'm looking for Ellison Thornhill. Have you seen him?"

"He lives in the monstrosity over there," Grant said, thumbing behind him.

"I wasn't sure if I'd find him there or the forest," the man said, dismounting.

There was something about his face and voice that seemed oddly familiar to PJ. "Pardon me," he said, "but have you ever stayed at the Weary Dragon Inn before?"

The man smiled, which changed the shape of his entire face. "I have. And you two boys look familiar to me, as well. Are you from Pigsend?"

A swell of happiness rose in PJ's chest. "PJ Norris and Grant Hamblin. We grew up in Pigsend."

"PJ Norris," the man said, rolling his name around in his mouth as if he were wracking his memory. "Grant… Wait a minute, you're Allen Mackey's fiancé's brother, right? Related to Dane Sterling?"

Grant's expression darkened at the mention of his taciturn elder relative who'd owned a farm outside Pigsend (and who'd also turned out to be in the king's inner circle). "Distantly."

The soldier chuckled, as if this were the most delightful thing in the world. "How wonderful to run into you young men. And in such a small place as Cheshireville. What brings you here?"

"We're investigating a mysterious happening in the forest for Ellison," PJ said.

"What kind of—"

"Andres!" Ellison called, jogging over after clearly having seen the group arriving from his office. "You're here! And you brought…well, wow. You brought a big contingent of soldiers. Why'd you do that?"

"They're simply ancillary," Andres said, waving him off. "They'll be camping out in the field while we conduct our business. You needn't worry about them."

Ellison gave them a nervous once-over. "V-very well then, why don't you come back to my house, and we can talk about everything."

"I'd actually like to see the forest," Andres said with a smile. "These boys said there was some kind of mysterious happening, though? Is there something I should be concerned about?"

"Nothing to worry about," Ellison said, although redness crept up his cheeks. "I'd be happy to take you there now." He looked back toward the contingent of soldiers. "Erm, I'm not sure there's enough room for—"

"Not to worry," Andres said, turning to his nearest soldier, who appeared to be a lieutenant. "Set up camp out here. I'll be back within the hour."

PJ and Grant trailed Andres and Ellison as they caught up, with Andres regaling Ellison with stories from King's Capital, including the wizards and mages and other powerful creatures who'd come out of hiding to return to their former glory. There were lots of names PJ had never heard, but one caught his attention.

"Shamus?" PJ called. "He's a wizard, right?"

"Almost," Andres said over his shoulder. "He was hiding out near Pigsend as an apprentice. Have you met him?"

"He came to the last village we stayed in," PJ said. "There were a trio of magical teens there.

Shamus said he'd set them up in King's Capital with magical training."

Andres nodded. "Lots of that happening. Kids who've either been in hiding or managed to avoid detection by the queen's people." He tilted his head. "How did Shamus find out about them?"

This was actually what PJ wanted to know, too. "Apparently, my—erm, grannies wrote to a friend who knows someone in King's Capital. Rita, Janet, and Gladys," he said, unsure if they ever gave a last name. "They're...dragon shifters, like me."

"Dragon shifters, eh?" Andres's eyes lit up with understanding. "I think I know who might've made that connection."

PJ and Grant shared a look. "Well?" Grant asked. "Who was it?"

"If it's who I'm thinking of, that particular person has requested anonymity," he said. "And I'd rather not divulge their identity without their consent."

PJ deflated. "Oh."

"The good news is that should you need to reach someone in King's Capital again, all you have to do is reach out to your...grandmothers, you said?" Andres asked.

PJ nodded. "Not by blood. They found me in Pigsend and, along with the innkeeper at the Weary Dragon, helped me through my first shift."

Andres nodded, a sparkling knowing in his gaze. "I see. And how are you now? I know dragon shifters can be quite temperamental when they don't travel with a pack." He looked at Grant. "You're not one, are you?"

"Absolutely not," Grant said, holding up his hands. "I'm just here to keep Peej from getting in trouble."

"I have a good amulet," PJ said, showing it to him. "You know a lot about dragon shifters. Do you know the grannies?"

"I've been around a long time," Andres said, nodding at the amulet. "Before the queen, the dragon shifters lived in the mountains just north of King's Capital. We'd see them on occasion, flying as a large pack. It was impressive, especially around the full moon. But of course, they were some of the first wiped out when the queen came to power." He smiled at PJ. "I'm glad the grannies found you before Dag Flanigan did."

At the name of his old magic-hunting nemesis, PJ shuddered. "You know about him?"

"Yes, I'm very familiar. I knew he was in Pigsend looking for a dragon shifter a few weeks before I passed through town. Suppose that was you, hm?"

PJ nodded. "He's not—"

"Trust me, he's never going to be a problem for you again," Andres said with a wink.

"Well, we certainly sorted him when he was in Pigsend. Valta—our friend—and I managed to trick him into leaving," Grant said, puffing out his chest. "Not that Dane would know about that. We weren't close."

"No, he didn't mention that, but he did tell me a lot about you and your sister, Victoria," Andres said. "Last I heard, you two were in Sheepsburg attending university."

Grant's cheeks colored. "Erm. Yeah. Decided that life wasn't for us." He shifted uncomfortably. "But Vicky is still in Sheepsburg. Probably engaged to her boyfriend—"

"Allen?" Andres asked with a frown.

"No, they broke up ages ago. She's seeing some rich guy." Grant shrugged.

"And how did you two end up all the way out here from Sheepsburg?" Andres asked.

"Peej got a letter from the grannies," Grant said quickly, perhaps to avoid the small detail about *his* involvement in them being evicted. "And we thought it was more important to look for more dragon shifters than fall asleep in class."

"Do you think there's a dragon shifter in Forest Den?" Andres asked, slowing slightly.

PJ shook his head. "Not that I can tell."

"So, and please don't take this question rudely, but if there isn't a dragon here, why haven't you moved on?" Andres's expression was genuine, as if he was trying to understand the duo.

"The grannies said that finding a dragon was going to be hard," PJ said. "That I was the only one they'd ever found in seven years of searching. But they also told me if someone was in trouble, I should stick around and help. I have these powers, and it'd be selfish not to use them whenever they could make someone's life better." He paused. "You know Bev, right? We've been trying to live by the idea of 'What would Bev do?'"

PJ didn't know how, but Andres's smile widened even more. "What would Bev do, indeed. I know she'd be quite proud of both of you." He turned to Ellison, who'd been watching the conversation with mild interest, his smile fading somewhat. "So, I take it these boys are here to help you with your holiday town plans? What kind of problems are you having?"

Ellison swallowed hard. "Well, it's nothing, really. But...these two *think* that maybe... I mean, it's probably not even that. I'm not even sure—"

"We think someone's trying to scare all the magical folks out of the village to sabotage Ellison's plans," Grant said.

"Really?" Andres's eyebrows shot up so high they would've disappeared under his hairline—if he'd had any.

"Erm, this is all just..." Ellison fidgeted. "I mean to say that..." He sighed. "I was hoping to have all this sorted before you got here, Andres. I don't want you not to invest in my town because... well, because someone has a vendetta against me."

"We've got some theories as to who it might be," PJ said. "Our prime suspect seems to have flown the coop for the moment. Which is good, because I don't think we'll see any surprises today. We're going to walk around the forest, if it'll let us, and keep looking for him."

"Good to hear," Andres said, then slowed. "What do you mean if the forest will let you?"

Ellison scowled at PJ and Grant. "It's a magical forest," Grant said, paying Ellison no mind. "Sometimes it lets us walk in happily. Other times, it kicks us out. It's quite temperamental. And it seems to be on the side of the culprit, at the moment. Something powerful is confusing it."

"That might be good news for me," Andres said, earning a look of surprise from everyone. "I confess, Ellison, I'm not just here to discuss investing in your holiday town. Right as the queen was coming to power, we heard rumors that something massive was in this forest. Something that could've helped the king then—but could really help him now as he tries to solidify his rule after the queen's reign. Perhaps if we can locate it, we might be able to solve both our problems."

The relief on Ellison's face was immediate, and he chattered away, telling Andres all about the town and the things he'd seen. But PJ and Grant slowed their gait, with PJ watching Andres with a new concern.

"What's up?" Grant asked.

"That encyclopedia said typhons were hunted for their powerful hearts," PJ said. "You don't think Andres is here to capture and…"

"He seems like a good guy," Grant said. "I don't think he'd want to hurt anyone."

PJ liked Andres, but something about his vagueness made him uneasy. Sure, the typhon was massive, but it wasn't the thing terrorizing the village. Andres had brought no fewer than thirty soldiers, and PJ didn't know how many of them had magic or what kind. Were they here to subdue the gentle giant?

They approached the forest, and to PJ's immense surprise, the trees opened a wide path for the group to pass through. The pressure, of course, was back, and Tim quieted down immediately, though he wasn't out of reach.

"Fascinating," Andres said as the trees moved. "Do you have some trick to get into the forest?"

"It knows me," Ellison said, looking quite relieved. "Part of my contribution would be to escort people to and from the forest. It's really not a long walk—"

"And that small village just outside," Andres said, thumbing behind him. "Does anyone still live there?"

"A couple folks," Ellison said, looking like he'd much rather avoid talking about them. "They haven't been very… They were quite…" He cleared his throat. "They were okay housing the queen's people. I don't know if they'd want to be involved in the holiday town. I don't even know if they should."

"If there's one thing I've learned over the past seven years," Andres said gently, "it's that we can't fault people for doing whatever they could to survive."

Ellison blinked at him. "But—"

"There were lots of folks who served the queen's people," Andres said, looking back at PJ and Grant. "You boys never faulted Bev for serving the queen's soldiers at the Weary Dragon, did you?"

PJ shook his head. "Never crossed my mind, to be honest."

"But we didn't think the king would be coming back, either," Grant added.

"Neither did I, and I was in the king's inner circle," Andres said with a chuckle. "But if those people have something to contribute, you should let them contribute, Ellison. No use holding grudges. The only way forward is together, you know?"

"They're the ones who turned my father in," Ellison said with a frown.

PJ, Grant, and Andres stopped walking. "What?" Andres asked.

"When the queen's people came through here looking for him," Ellison said, his gaze stoic, "he was hiding at the abandoned inn. Someone tipped the queen's soldiers." He turned to Andres. "There were only a handful of people who knew where he was—and they're all in that town over there. I'm sure they got paid for it, too."

Andres nodded in understanding. "You don't know who—"

"I know enough," Ellison huffed, walking forward. "And the last thing I want is for those people to benefit from my hard work. So let's go."

The walk into the village was awkwardly silent after that, with PJ mulling over what Ellison had said. No wonder he had such a grudge against the people in the village. But they hadn't mentioned it, so was it really true?

The village was full of anxious energy when the quartet arrived, but Andres didn't seem to notice any of it. He inhaled deeply, looking around with a smile as he took in the sight of it.

"I've been to a few of these magical enclaves

now," he said to Ellison. "But this one is, by far, the most open and spacious."

"It didn't used to be," Ellison said. "There were more people, more tree houses. About three quarters of the town left when the queen was overthrown. Most of the trees returned to the forest, too. But those that stayed…" He finally lost the remainder of his angst. "Well, we've made some amazing little houses for people to live in. Come, I'll show them to you, and we can meet some of the townsfolk."

PJ and Grant let Ellison lead Andres away and took the opportunity to head back toward the edge of the forest to talk. PJ chose the side of the forest near the tree he'd climbed the night before, as he knew the house was vacant, and he had an idea what he wanted to do next.

"Well, at least now we know why Ellison hates the townsfolk," Grant said. "He couldn't have just come out and said that up front, could he?"

"Seems like it's a painful subject for him," PJ said, glancing upward. From down here, he could only just make out the wooden walkway—but only because he was looking for it. "I think we should go back up there. Our culprit doesn't know we know about it, so maybe if we climb up there—"

"I'm not doing that," Grant said with a frown.

"Come on," PJ said with a sigh, putting his hand on the tree. "It's not that hard."

Based on Grant's whining, it was *quite* hard, but eventually, the boys climbed all the way up the tree until they found the walkway. Grant whistled loudly as he put his hand on the vines suspending the bridge, knocking the wooden plank with his knuckle from the safety of the nearby tree branch.

"Someone put in a lot of work for this," Grant said. "Are you sure it's safe?"

"It was sturdy enough to hold my weight," PJ said, climbing onto the walkway cautiously. "C'mon, let's—"

"Can't we just wait up here?" Grant said, pushing the walkway gently with the tip of his toe. "I mean, we can see the entire town from up here. If our culprit—"

"Are you afraid of heights or something?" PJ asked, turning to walk in the direction he had the night before. After a few minutes, the walkway swayed as Grant joined him.

~

PJ moved with a bit more confidence and swiftness than the night before. He didn't know if he'd come across the typhon sleeping or not—how much did they sleep?—but he was hoping he'd find Harold in the tree house, at least. Grant's theory seemed the most solid, especially after Ellison had confirmed most of what Grant had suspected. But PJ still needed undeniable proof that Harold wasn't just friends with the typhon but that he wanted everyone out of the town. And there was something holding him back from saying they'd found their culprit.

"Okay, that's not creepy at all," Grant said from behind PJ as the tree house came into view. "Why is it so high?"

"Just be quiet," PJ said. "We don't know who's waiting for us in there."

They crouched low, moving slowly across the walkway and making little sound. PJ tried to send Tim ahead to look, but as usual, his dragon was confined to his head. PJ got to the wraparound porch and clambered to the wall, hiding under the open window and gesturing for Grant to join him.

"Okay, now what?" Grant whispered.

PJ put his finger to his mouth and craned his neck as much as he could while still staying hidden. There was a telltale *thump thump*, followed by Harold's clear voice.

"I ain't got no more of that for you. Gonna have to be slim pickings for a while yet, eh?" A pause. "Well, because those two young whippersnappers have turned the entire town against me—and Ellison! I'm pretty sure he's gonna fire me for real this time." Another pause. "Yes, I know he tried that. But I think he might call the law on me."

"Who's he talking to?" Grant mouthed.

PJ shrugged, but when he peeked inside, Harold was out on the other side of the porch, and he didn't seem to have his usual assortment of gardening equipment. So PJ jumped to his feet, gesturing to Grant, and walked right into the tree house.

"Hi, Harold," he said.

"What are you two doing here?" Harold growled, jumping to his feet. He clutched for something—anything—but all he found was the same teddy bear PJ had the night before.

"We're not here to hurt you," PJ said, holding up his hands. "But we need you to tell us the truth: Are you the one sabotaging Ellison's town?"

Harold's bushy brows knitted together. "No, I ain't. But I hear I'm the one gettin' blamed for it anyway, so why don't you just take me away?"

"Who's here with yo—Oh my *goooooooosh*," Grant bellowed, stumbling backward as a pair of warm brown eyes the size of wagons peered into the tree house.

Chapter Nineteen

PJ had, of course, seen it from afar, but there was nothing like staring into the face of a creature whose mouth was bigger than PJ was tall. The head, which was as bulbous and knobby as the ink drawing in that encyclopedia had suggested, scraped the very top of the canopy, and the trees themselves moved out of the way to avoid knocking into him. His hair was gray, plastered to his scalp like he was in dire need of a wash. His eyebrows were bushy and unkempt; his pale skin wrinkled around his cheeks and sagged a bit at the jowls. He didn't seem to carry any extra weight, though his arms were thick at the forearms and his bare feet were as large as the tree house PJ currently stood in.

Although the typhon cut an imposing figure, PJ didn't feel scared at all. There was still that all-encompassing feeling of *power,* but as PJ acclimated, he found it much less intimidating than he had at first.

PJ, unfortunately, was the only one who had this feeling, as Grant was plastered against the back wall of the tree house, paler than PJ had ever seen him before.

"W-w-what is that?" he stammered, swallowing. "P-Peej?"

"His name is Stone," Harold barked. "And he ain't gonna hurt you two. Ain't never hurt anyone, I tell ya, and that the two of you are walking around saying otherwise is—"

"Aren't *you* the one who told us on our very first day that the typhon could crush us?" Grant said, casting him a dirty look.

A tinge of color darkened Harold's cheeks. "Well, I's hoping you two would get the hint and leave. I could tell you were trouble from the moment I laid eyes on ya. Hovering around the manor like you were. And now here you are, coming with your weapons and your fire to run my friend out of his home."

"We're doing nothing of the sort," PJ said, glaring at him. "But you've got to stop harassing the people of Forest Den."

Harold made a face. "I ain't harassing nobody."

"Aren't you?" Grant asked. "PJ found Bill's axe in the trees next to the little walkway that goes right to your tree house."

"I don't know nothing about an axe," Harold said. "And this walkway's been here since my grandfather built it ages ago."

That was news to PJ. "Really? It's that old?"

Harold nodded. "My family's been living around this place for generations. My great-grandfather was the first one to meet Stone. When he started working for the first Thornhill."

The giant smiled and nodded.

"We sorta protected him, you know? The magical folks came and went from Thornhill Manor, and we worried they'd find Stone. Maybe think he was too big to let live, or that their own precious magic was in danger. My grandfather made me swear when he brought me here as a boy that I'd never let anyone hurt him."

"Because people used to hunt their hearts for power," PJ said softly.

Harold nodded. "Stone's one of the last typhons around, you know? Not right what they did to 'em. And I'd be darned if I let anyone find him."

"Then why'd you mention him to *us*?" Grant muttered. "And the townsfolk said you'd been talking about it to everyone who passed through—"

"If someone thought I was serious," Harold said, "they'd have to contend with the forest. And if the queen's own soldiers couldn't get past the first root, I doubt someone who wanted to hurt Stone could, either."

"Okay, so it's not Harold," Grant said. "And it's clearly not Stone. But someone wants everyone to *think* it's Stone. Why?"

The typhon began moving his eyes as if he had something to say. Harold shook his head. "I don't understand you when you're talking like that, Stone. And these boys don't hear you."

"Wait," PJ said. "Tim probably could."

"Who's Tim?" Harold asked.

PJ stepped toward the typhon, calling on his dragon. To his surprise, Tim wasn't just available to chat, but the pressure keeping his dragon powers contained relented completely. PJ's eyes burned as the dragon magic took over, the colors of the forest inverting from green to purple and the giant before him turning a lighter shade of pink. Through his dragon's eyes, he spotted the glowing center of magic that PJ had felt when he'd seen the typhon from afar. He lifted his gaze to meet the typhon's and found the giant wearing a friendly smile.

Hello, came a new voice in PJ's mind, one that was deep, gravelly, and, most of all, quite pleasant. *I*

Stone.

I Tim.

You dragon.

You typhon.

I friend.

I friend.

The conversation continued in monosyllabic fashion until Tim had conveyed who PJ was, why they were there, and asked the giant if he had any idea who was terrorizing the town.

I like town, said the typhon. *Funny creatures. Nice. No bother.*

Someone bother.

Stone frowned, as if he had no idea. *Why?*

Human nonsense.

PJ snorted. "You aren't wrong."

"What in the world is he doing?" Harold asked. "He's just standing there, talking to himself."

"Let the dragon do his thing," Grant replied.

I help find. Me and Harold no bother. Like tiny creatures. The typhon's massive lips turned downward. *Forest confused.*

Why confuse?

Something confuse. Tiny creature make confuse. I see.

Why?

Stone shrugged. *Human nonsense.*

PJ blinked away the dragon magic and told

Grant and Harold the gist of the conversation. "Who has the power to befuddle this powerful forest?"

Harold glowered. "One of them magical folks in the village, I'm sure."

"Only Ingrid can talk to the trees, and even she had trouble near that footprint. But she doesn't give me the sense she's hiding something."

"People can surprise you, Peej," Grant said. "Well, we've found the typhon and we've found our only suspect, and neither one is involved. What's our next move?"

PJ rubbed his chin. "We should head back to the village. Find Andres and Ellison."

"You gonna tell him about Stone?" Harold asked.

"No, your secret's safe with us," PJ said with a smile, thinking about Andres, and how he was searching for something powerful in the forest. "The world's changed, but even I'm still nervous about telling people what I really am. Besides that, I can see the power in Stone's heart, and I don't want anyone to get any funny ideas about him."

Harold relaxed. "Thank you."

"And we'll be sure to tell your boss that you're not the one causing the ruckus," Grant said. "Though it would be swell if you could tell us who it might be." He turned to the gardener. "Who else would know about your little walkway?"

"Nobody that I know," he said. "Can't guarantee one of those magical things who lived in the forest didn't find it, though. If you're looking for someone to blame, I'd point at them first."

"They'd want to cause trouble in their own village so their neighbors would leave?" PJ asked.

"Well, maybe not." Harold deflated. "But they shouldn't have invaded the forest. And now their welcome has worn out. There are plenty of other places for them to go. Shouldn't be here. And that Ellison shouldn't turn this forest into some kind of touristy town, either. The kinds of people who'd be coming and going. Can't trust 'em." He shifted. "I'm not as young as I used to be, and I ain't got any kids."

PJ smiled, sensing his concern. "You know, Stone's lived in this forest a long time, including the seven years that the small village was here. They never saw hide nor hair of him. And they didn't go seeking him, either. I think that, if Ellison's plan goes through, the forest would continue to protect him from anyone. Besides that... I bet Ellison would love to help you."

Harold's eyebrows drew together in anger. "I ain't telling that rich boy nothin."

"Well, maybe someone else, then," Grant said. "But I think Peej is right. This forest is gigantic—

and powerful. Tourists or not, I think Stone's gonna be safe." He quirked a brow at the typhon. "I can't see how he wouldn't be, the size he is."

"You'd be surprised," Harold said. "And I'd be grateful if you wouldn't mention him to anyone."

"Of course," PJ said with a nod. "It was, erm, nice to meet you, Stone."

The typhon just grinned.

~

"You know, whoever our culprit is has no idea what a typhon is really like, do they?" Grant mused. "Clearly, they were just going by what Harold had said."

"I wonder who was reading that encyclopedia, then?" PJ asked.

"Another mystery." Grant shrugged. "We didn't ask Harold about the attic or the stuff that was stolen. If he's close with the forest, maybe he can help us locate it."

"I don't think it's related," PJ said. "I mean, if you've got someone powerful enough to befuddle a forest, why do you need a bag of magic tricks?"

"I mean, why do you need to throw a rock if you have a sword?" Grant asked.

PJ stopped and looked at him, confused. "What?"

"You'd throw a rock if your opponent's too far to hit with the sword," Grant said, as if that were an obvious answer. "Which is a long-winded way of saying, sometimes the crude weapon works better than the sophisticated one, depending on the circumstances. If you're trying to scare people out of town, why not use smoke and mirrors instead of using your own magic? Kishan said he could fool even the most powerful wizards. I'm sure it's probably the same for a town full of magical people."

PJ turned back around to keep walking, thinking to himself. "It's not as if there are many people left for us to put on the suspect list. We've got a handful of folks in Cheshireville, none of whom have been able to enter the forest. A handful of folks in Forest Den, none of whom would have any motive to want their neighbors to leave."

"Maybe it's not about getting them to leave permanently, just to get Ellison off his holiday spot plans," Grant said.

"Ellison's not going to be able to buy them any more supplies. If they aren't making their own gold to buy their own, how are they supposed to keep living there?"

"I didn't say whoever's doing it was farsighted, just that they could want to sabotage the plans only," Grant said. "We probably should see if that Hilde woman really left. Maybe she just made a show of it, but she's really hiding out at the

Cheshireville Inn until Ellison gives up."

"Maybe," PJ said as they drew closer. "Well, the good news is that befuddled or not, the forest has let Tim come out. I'm basically back to full strength."

"Do you think Stone is the one controlling the forest?" Grant asked.

PJ shook his head. "No, I think the forest is friends with Stone. And Stone is incredibly powerful. But even he's not powerful enough to cow every individual tree in the forest to his whims. Ingrid said they all have their own opinions, even if they're in agreement with each other."

"There's the village," Grant said as the village clearing appeared ahead. "Now, how are we gonna get down without breaking our necks?"

I help.

"AAAAAAAAAHHHHHHHHHHHHH."

PJ—or Tim, rather—hadn't given Grant time to argue, simply grabbing him by the waist and jumping off the tree. PJ, who'd done this jump before, was still afraid, but with Tim fully able to control his body, the pulse spike was at a minimum. They floated down softly, PJ dropping Grant, who crumpled to the ground in a heaving, panicked mess.

"Don't do that again!" Grant bellowed at him as he clutched his chest.

"You want down," Tim said through PJ's mouth.

PJ blinked away the magic in his eyes and shook it from his body, clearing his throat. "Yeah, he did that to me last night, too. Not a fan."

Grant scowled at him. "Give a guy a *warning* next time."

"Are you two…all right?"

Andres and Ellison, along with Bill, Pat, and Ingrid, had all come running at the sound of Grant's terrified screaming, and stood a few paces away, watching the boys curiously.

"And where'd you come from?" Pat asked, looking up at the canopy. "Were you climbing in the trees?"

"Yes," PJ said, not wanting to give away the existence of the walkway. "We found Bill's axe up there last night."

Bill's brows rose, and he tilted his head skyward. "How in the world did it get up there?"

"Long story," PJ said, glancing at Ellison, who was nodding toward Andres with a nervous smile. "How'd you like the town, Andres?"

"I think Ellison's got a great business plan," Andres said with a firm nod. "Especially if it helps the magical folks get back on their feet, I'm sure the king would love to send a grant or two your way to help with setup costs."

Ellison exhaled loudly, as if a gigantic weight

had just been lifted off his chest. "That's incredible. Thank you, Andres."

"Is this the same kind of grant the king's been handing out all over the country?" PJ asked.

Andres nodded. "The queen had hoarded as much gold as she could, along with many other things, and the king's been eager to ensure it's redistributed to the people who need it most. Something like this, which would provide a leg up for magical folks to start their businesses? That's exactly the sort of thing he wants to invest in."

The Forest Den folks shared a smile. "That's amazing," Ingrid said. "So Ellison could start advertising for people to come?"

"Well, we probably need to..." Ellison began, looking at PJ and Grant.

But before PJ could answer, commotion on the other side of town drew his attention. It took PJ a moment to realize that it was a group of people he hadn't expected—the small group of Cheshireville merchants. How they got in was a mystery to PJ, but clearly they were determined to find people they wanted to see.

"Ellison Thornhill, you've gone too far!" Brennan barked, pointing his finger.

"What's the meaning of this?" Ellison asked, looking around. "What's wrong?"

"You!" Orlena looked ready to burst into tears.

"You and these…*soldiers!* They need to leave. Right now!"

"They've ruined *everything!*" Adonna cried.

"What's going on?" Andres asked, stepping forward. "If my soldiers have done anything that's offended or hurt anyone in this town, I will do everything in my power to ensure they're punished for it."

"Your soldiers have *arrested* our only regular merchant customers!" Ulysses said, his face bright red. "Roe and Oscar. All they did was come to town."

"A-arrested?" Ellison gaped. "Why did they—"

"Because they're not merchants," Andres said with a satisfied smile. "They're some of Queen Meandra's most dangerous spies. Ones I've been very eager to arrest for the better part of a year."

"Spies?" The nonmagical quartet gaped at Andres. Even Ellison, who'd probably had run-ins with the merchants when he dared show his face around the village, looked blindsided.

"We'd gotten a tip that they were moving in this area," Andres said. "As I said, there have been lots of threads we had to put down to deal with the queen, and now that things are getting back to normal, we can pick them up. Oscar and Roe—or Joe and Albert Wickles, as they're really called—did loads of damage in these parts as spies for the queen."

"I-impossible," Adonna said. "They've never… They've been so kind to us. What could they possibly have done for H-Her Majesty?"

"We didn't know they were spies until after the queen was overthrown," Andres said. "Before the queen, they'd infiltrated Thornhill Manor, gathering intelligence about each of the powerful wizards and mages who came to be entertained."

"What were they still doing around here, then?" PJ asked.

"Yeah, they've been coming to town every couple of days for years," Brennan said. "What could they possibly need with our small town?"

"That's the question, isn't it?" Andres gestured toward the forest. "Why don't we head out to the encampment and see what these spies have to say?"

Chapter Twenty

The crowd begrudgingly agreed, with the townsfolk trailing Andres and talking amongst themselves.

"How could they be spies?" Adonna whispered to Orlena. "They're the ones who told people in other towns about my custards. Were those people spies, too?"

"I just can't believe it," Orlena said with a firm shake of her head. "They have to have the wrong people. Seven years is a long time. There's no way… Absolutely no way."

"How sure are you that you have the right people?" Brennan asked the lieutenant. "I mean, it just seems—"

"Quite sure," the lieutenant said. "They confessed upon arrest."

The townsfolk shared another concerned look.

"How could they be evil if they were so good to us?" Orlena said.

"People contain multitudes," Andres said with a shrug. "And the queen's spies would absolutely be keen to get on the good side of local folks like yourselves. You'd probably tell them about anything curious happening in town, or if any magicals were sniffing around, wouldn't you?"

The townspeople stared at him as if he had two heads.

"But they ran in the same circles as my father," Ellison said, also seeming confused by the revelation. "How did *he* not know?"

"No one knew," Andres said, heavily.

Ellison's pace slowed, and PJ joined him, sensing he might need a friendly ear.

"What's on your mind?"

"I can't believe… all this time…" Ellison licked his lips. "I feel like a fool."

"We can only work with the information we have," PJ said with a shrug. "And speaking of that, I don't think Harold's our culprit anymore."

Ellison looked up at him, frowning. "Well, then who the heck is it?"

PJ lifted a shoulder. "Maybe Roe and Oscar will have something to add. Perhaps they're our missing piece."

The lieutenant led them all the way back to the Cheshireville Inn, where they found a dining room full of soldiers, with Roe and Oscar heavily shackled at one of the tables. They sneered at the folks coming in—mostly at Andres—and looked completely different than the casual, carefree merchants who'd munched on delicious custards and shared a meal with PJ and Grant that first night.

Now, PJ could absolutely see the cunning behind their dark eyes in the way they surveyed the room for a means of escape. Tim growled deep in PJ's mind, the true measure that they'd been completely wrong about these two.

"Well?" Andres said, crossing his arms in front of his chest. "Having you two in chains has certainly been a long time coming. Do you have anything to say for yourselves?"

"Only that we wish Her Majesty had been a little less lenient on you." Even Roe's voice had taken on an unfamiliar tone, one that was full of loathing and intellect.

"You've deceived all the people in this town," Andres said. "Made them believe you were merchants when you were clearly not—"

"Oh, what? We gave them money when no one

else would?" Oscar snorted, sitting back in his chair and smirking. "The king hasn't shown up to help them."

"How charitable," Andres said. "Unless our dearly departed queen specifically told you two to hang around this town to help it, I can't imagine you had another goal in mind." His smile widened. "Like perhaps trying to find a particular amulet that might've gone missing around the time Marley Thornhill was arrested?"

Ellison stood up straighter. "What are you talking about?"

"One of the King's Quartet was here when the queen's people attacked," Andres said. "To protect their magic, they hid their very powerful amulet somewhere in the forest. Didn't work out for them too well, but rumor has it their amulet is still in the forest."

Oscar and Roe shifted.

"Wait, are you two the ones behind all the monster nonsense?" Ellison asked, standing.

"What are you talking about?" Oscar asked.

"The past three weeks, half the town's been scared away by someone pretending to be a monster," Ellison said, his cheeks turning blotchy. "Was it you two? To scare the people out of town to find the amulet?"'

The two shared a look of genuine confusion.

"Wasn't us," Oscar said.

"The forest never let us get so much as a toe into its boundaries," Roe replied. "Though we certainly tried."

"Especially after the queen took over," Oscar said. "Could feel the magic creeping in when I slept in the bed upstairs. It didn't want us anywhere near it."

"This amulet," PJ said to Andres, "would it be powerful enough to confuse the forest?"

Andres frowned. "What do you mean?"

"I mean, if someone were to wield it inside the forest, could it influence the forest to do certain things?" The wheels turned in PJ's mind. "Some kind of powerful force seems to be mixing up the forest. We thought it might be a person with that kind of power, but what if it's just the amulet?" He turned to the two spies. "Where is it buried?"

"No clue," Roe said with a knowing smirk. When one of Andres's soldiers advanced, he lost his confidence. "I mean that. We just know one of the Quartet buried it somewhere in the forest. One of the last things they did before our side got to them."

"Who was around that night?" PJ asked, looking at Ellison. "You? Your father?"

Ellison shook his head. "I wasn't around. I was at school. Away. All I know is there was a big party, then the next thing I know, everyone was arrested.

They didn't catch my father at first, but then *someone*—" He cast a dirty look at the townsfolk "—ratted him out."

"It certainly wasn't us!" Orlena gasped, hand to her chest. "And it's quite outrageous of you to even insinuate—"

"Then who did?" Ellison said. "You four knew where my father was hiding, I—" He turned to the spies, who'd suddenly started looking everywhere else. "It was you. You're the ones who..." He took a step back, like his whole world was turning upside down. "My father trusted you. He thought you were his friends. And you..."

"You see why I was so keen to get my hands on them," Andres said gently.

Ellison's face had turned bright red and his fists shook. He turned wordlessly on his heel and stormed out of the inn.

"All this time... Ellison thought *we* were the ones to betray his father?" Brennan said, looking astonished. "We would never."

"We loved Marley," Adonna said. "You two..." She walked up to Oscar and Roe and scowled at them. "I regret every single custard I ever sold you."

"Hear, hear," Brennan said. "Glad you're being taken away to suffer for your crimes."

Ulysses and Orlena nodded fervently. "Oh, but we should check on poor Ellison," Orlena said. "I'm sure he's upset—"

"I'll go check on him," PJ turned to leave then paused. "But since these soldiers are camping out in the fields—and I assume you won't be leaving today, right, Andres?"

"Correct."

"Then why don't you whip up a batch of those custards?" PJ said to Adonna. "And perhaps see if there's any laundry to do. Or if they'd like a cider to wash down some dinner. They're headed back to King's Capital soon, I bet. I'm sure they'd love to tell their friends about your town here—especially if it's going to be a tourist spot."

The townsfolk lit up with excitement, especially as Adonna began counting the people (very purposefully *overlooking* Oscar and Roe) to see how many custards she'd have to provide. PJ and Grant left them to it, excusing themselves as they headed out to find Ellison.

He wasn't too far ahead, walking toward the forest and still looking like he would rather not be bothered. As PJ and Grant caught up with him, he was murmuring to himself.

"I can't believe… all this time…" Ellison shook his head. "I don't know what makes me feel worse, that I was so quick to judge the townsfolk or the depths of Roe and Oscar's betrayal." He shook his head. "They were good friends with my father, you know. But I suppose that's what you do when you're spying for the queen."

"I'm sorry," PJ said. "But you can take some comfort in them seeing justice, finally."

"And you won't have to hate the townsfolk anymore, either," Grant said with a wry grin.

"Whether they'll forgive me is another story," Ellison said. "But perhaps, as Andres said, gold is gold. And we can come to some sort of..." He rubbed his face. "But what was that about Harold? You said he wasn't the culprit?"

Their conversation stopped abruptly when Audra and Delaney, along with Ingrid, Pat, and Bill, came bolting out of the forest, their faces white with terror. PJ ran as fast as his legs could carry him to see what might've happened.

"Another tree limb," Audra said, clutching her chest. "Nearly took Ingrid out with it."

"Then..." Ingrid looked on the verge of tears. "Then a *tree fell.*"

"What does that matter?" Grant asked, folding his arms across his chest. "It's a forest. Trees fall all the time, don't they?"

Ingrid gasped at him as if he'd spoken blasphemy.

"There's a vile monster trying to hurt all of us," Audra said, looking between PJ and Grant. "And you two were supposed to stop it!"

"Ellison, we can't stay in that town any longer," Bill said. "I know you were trying to help us, but it's just too dangerous. We can't risk our lives."

Ellison shook his head, gesturing back toward the town. "But I just got a grant. I'm going to be able to finish fixing up the place, advertise, bring in new people. We have to… We can't give up now."

"I'm sorry, Ellison, but it's time," Pat said with a shake of his head. "You know I'm as loyal to you as they come, but I can't risk my neck, either. I think we'll all head back in there, pack up the rest of our stuff and—"

"Wait…" PJ furrowed his brow. "Nobody's in the forest right now?"

They shared a look, as if that was the least important thing to discuss.

"Where are you going?" Grant called as PJ bolted toward the trees.

"To find our culprit."

For the first time, PJ walked up to the forest alone and the path opened up for him. But as he drew closer to the village, he found his path blocked, and the presence of the forest pushed him back until he was back out on the plain again, where Grant was waiting.

"What's wrong?" Grant asked.

"The forest is confused again," PJ said, looking

around with a frown. "We need to get in there. Our villain wanted the village empty. They got their wish. Now we need to get in there and see who it is."

He walked toward the forest again, but the force of magic pushed him backward once more.

"Are you gonna have to blow a hole through it?" Grant asked.

PJ had an idea. "No. But we're going to have to hurry. I'm not sure how much time we have."

With Grant trailing him, PJ ran toward the forest, though this time around the edge. It hadn't taken him that long before, but he still put on a burst of speed. He hoped his previous conversations with the typhon would grease the wheels with this part of the forest, because if not, he wasn't sure what he was going to do.

He had a good guess where Harold had summoned the typhon the day before and walked up to the edge. "Stone?" he called. "Are you there?"

"Oh, you aren't..." Grant said with a swallow. "Really?"

"Might be the fastest way to get there," PJ said. "Stone?"

Let me. Tim said. *Stone?*

PJ held his breath and waited. Then, a smile grew on his face as the trees shifted out of the way, and the massive creature emerged from the trees, tilting his head expectantly at the duo.

"I think…" Grant whispered, his voice filled with trepidation. "I underestimated how big this thing is."

We need village, Tim said. *Forest no like.*

I can take.

Stone held out his flat palm, the same way he had with Harold, and PJ and Grant clambered on top, with PJ practically dragging Grant behind him. They both struggled to keep their footing as they rose into the sky.

Stone lifted his hand so they were eye to eye with him. *I take village?*

Just to tree house, Tim said. *We want sneak.*

Understood.

"Whoa!" Grant cried as Stone turned to walk into the forest.

But the giant seemed to take the utmost care, clearly used to carrying smaller creatures like Harold. PJ was brave enough to look down past the typhon's wrinkled hand to the forest below, amazed to watch the trees move out of their way, just as Harold had said. It was an incredible symbiotic relationship, and it made something in PJ's soul very happy. The tree house appeared ahead, and Stone lowered his hand to be level with the wraparound porch, allowing PJ and Grant to hop off.

"Thank you," PJ said before realizing he'd

spoken. "Erm, Tim?"

He know. Now let's go.

"Wait a minute," Grant said, realizing too late what he'd signed up for. "Wait, are we going to have to fly down again? Because I'm pretty sure I *already* said—"

"Stay here with Stone, then," PJ said, impatiently. "We don't have a lot of time."

Without waiting for Grant to argue, PJ barreled down the walkway, hoping that the culprit hadn't snatched the amulet and run. But when he arrived at the village, his heart sank as he found it completely empty. With Tim's vision, he scanned each of the homes, looking for signs of either the amulet or the culprit.

There.

He jumped off the walkway, letting Tim's magic waft him down to the ground. He landed softly and padded across the town as the sound of frantic searching reached his ears.

"Where is it… Come on, I know it's around here somewhere…"

"Looking for something, Kishan?"

Chapter Twenty-One

Kishan jumped and turned around, his eyes going wide. He held a shovel in one hand and had dirt smeared on his face. "W-what are you doing here?"

"I could ask you the same question," PJ said. "Aren't you worried about the typhon? It definitely scared everyone else out of town in a hurry. Which is odd, because it doesn't usually make noise at this time of day, you know?"

Kishan swallowed. "I'm sure it won't bother me. But it might bother you, dragon shifter. Probably drawn to you. Harold said as much, if you'll recall."

"You know, Harold seems to have embellished a

few facts about them," PJ said with a shrug. "They're really quite peaceful. Don't like to be seen or bothered. And they actually wear shoes, if you can believe it." He chuckled. "Guess that footprint was dug by the same person who doesn't know typhons don't roar or talk."

Kishan licked his lips.

"We found an encyclopedia at Ellison's house with all this good information in it, but clearly, you just skimmed it for the basics," PJ said with a bright smile. "And listened to Harold too much."

"What are you talking about?" Kishan, to his credit, seemed to have regained his mask and looked unbothered by these revelations.

"Well, you know, using your bag of magical tricks to scare the town into leaving so you could hunt for the amulet without them knowing," PJ said. "That is why you're here, isn't it? You're looking for the amulet that King's Quartet person left behind, right?"

Kishan let out a laugh then turned around and bolted, throwing the shovel as he went. PJ deftly avoided the projectile and followed, but before Kishan could get very far, he was met by not just the Forest Den folks, but the Cheshireville set and Andres, all led by Ingrid. They took in the wild-eyed innkeeper with surprise as PJ strolled up behind him.

"Kishan?" Brennan said. "I thought you were delivering my cider casks?"

"Erm, I…" Kishan's gaze darted around. "I'm not—"

"Are *you* the one behind all this?" Ellison cried, his face red. "How could you?"

"It's not—" Kishan said. "It's Harold. I swear. I saw him with the typhon just the other day—"

"How *dare* you!" Harold bellowed from somewhere up above.

The trees parted, and someone screamed as the typhon emerged from the trees, frowning and looking most upset. Cupped in his hands were Harold and Grant, who clearly regretted his alternative way to the ground. The latter climbed down clumsily, while the old man hopped down with surprising agility and marched over to Kishan with his rake up in the air.

"I've been protectin' this forest my whole life, and you dare tell these people I had anything to do with them feeling unwelcome?" Harold continued. "Blamin' me for stealing your magical stuff? I would *never!*"

Kishan ran toward the townsfolk, who seemed to see him in a different light now.

"What's going on, Kishan?" Brennan asked. "Are you a queen's spy, too?"

"Queen's…what?" Kishan blinked. "The queen's

out of power—"

"Oscar and Roe had been keeping some secrets from us, it turns out," Adonna said, lifting her nose higher. "Are you about to tell us you weren't really a magician but some kind of...I don't know, master thief?"

Everyone had crowded around the innkeeper, who seemed to be searching for a friendly face. When he found none, he shook his head, his shoulders dropping. "Fine, all right. I'm behind all of it," Kishan said. "But I'm not a master thief. I'm just a guy hoping to get lucky."

"How so?" Andres asked with mild interest.

Kishan glanced at the soldier, perhaps realizing his admission wasn't the smartest move in front of the law. "Well, seven years ago, I was working at Thornhill Manor when the queen's soldiers ambushed everyone. Found myself in a room with one of the wizards, who was acting all squirrelly. I think he got hit with something..." He shuddered.

"Philandro, right?" Andres said, watching Kishan with a frown. "You were one of the last people to see him alive, then. You took his amulet?"

Kishan kicked the ground then nodded. "He gave it to me." His voice dropped as he recalled the memory. "Philandro really liked my magical stuff. Said it was neat how I could fool him, as he could always see through magic. He thought I could fool the queen's folks…"

"And you did," PJ said. "You brought it to the forest."

"First time it ever let me in," Kishan said. "I could hear the trees and told 'em to forget they saw me, forget about the amulet, and if anyone asks, not to tell 'em anything. I was panicking, of course, thinking I'd be caught by the queen's soldiers the moment I left, but no one ever knew I had it or what happened to it." He exhaled, perhaps recalling the fear he'd felt in the moment. "But the soldiers left, and the town got real quiet for the most part. I didn't think it was right to leave, just in case someone came back looking for it. So I got the inn set up so I could keep an eye on the forest." He sighed. "Then the queen was gone, the forest opened, and I realized an entire village had sprung up on top of where I'd buried that amulet."

"Did you try to dig it up?" PJ asked.

He shook his head. "Philandro told me it was important, and all kinds of unsavory creatures could try to take it off my hands. But I was sure nobody'd found it, and I figured I could wait until everyone cleared out. But then, a handful of folks stuck around."

"Why did you start a ruckus now, then?" Ellison asked.

"Because he found out about your holiday

plans," PJ said. "And if he didn't act fast—"

"It had nothing to do with Ellison's plans. I saw the letter from him." Kishan pointed to Andres. "I'd heard from the soldiers that the king was giving all kinds of rewards for recovering artifacts and the like. And knew if I was gonna get it back in the right person's hands, I needed to get it soon."

A flicker of surprise shot over PJ. "The right person's…?"

"You were friends with Philandro. It would be safe with you." Kishan stared at the ground. "And, you know, maybe give me a little reward for my effort."

"Why not just *tell* us?" Ingrid asked, exasperated. "We could've helped you find what you were looking for. There was no point in scaring us half to death."

"I've seen magical creatures like you," Kishan said with a glare. "They were all over Thornhill Manor. You'd sooner steal it than let me sell it. And I'd have no recourse. Besides that…I wanted to make sure I got it back to Andres. And, well… Well, I thought you folks would scare a bit easier than you did. I didn't need you to be gone forever, just long enough for me to get the amulet." He sighed. "Then you could come back, Ellison could have his holiday town, and I could sell the inn and retire somewhere nice with…my reward." He glanced at Andres, who snorted.

"What about us?" Adonna said, stepping forward. "You'd abandon us like that?"

"You'll have plenty of business," Kishan said. "You wouldn't need the inn anymore. Ellison would take good care of you." He sighed. "It was all gonna work out so well." He glared at PJ and Grant. "If it wasn't for you nosy kids meddling in my affairs."

"Well, this has all been very enlightening," Andres said, sounding a bit exhausted. "But if Philandro's amulet is somewhere in this forest, I'd like to have it so I can return it to the king's vault. There are other wizards vying for a position in the Quartet, and they would very much appreciate having the wizard's assistant back."

I help.

PJ jumped as Stone's voice echoed through his mind. The typhon leaned forward and dug his long fingers into the rocky ground, digging until a small box popped out of it.

Andres approached the box, kneeling and unlatching it.

Immediately, the hair on PJ's arms rose, and Tim roared in appreciation. It was, by far, the most powerful thing PJ had ever been around. His amulet warmed in response, and his eyes burned as Tim thrashed in his mind.

Someone grabbed him by the arm, bringing him

back to the present, and PJ turned to see Grant's worried expression staring back at him. He blinked away the magic, realizing Andres had closed the box again, and made an immediate decision to stay *as far away* from that thing as humanly possible.

"That's it," Ingrid said, a little breathlessly. "That's the thing that's been causing the trees to be so ornery." She glared at it. "Take it out of here. The trees want to be rid of it."

"Happy to," Andres said, tucking the box safely under his arm.

"Well?" Kishan cleared his throat. "Do I get a reward for keeping it safe?"

"Hm," Andres said, looking around. "I do think a reward should be given, yes. But I also think a penance should be paid for the harm you've caused these poor folks. Scaring them out of their homes and the like." He turned to Ellison. "I will get this back to the king and see what he wishes to pay. Can you ensure that the money is evenly divided amongst the people here?"

"Give it to Ellison," Pat said, waving him off. "He used up all his gold to keep us alive when the queen was in power. We could never repay him otherwise."

Ellison smiled at him. "How about this: I'll use that gold to ensure this is the most well-advertised holiday spot ever. There'll be hundreds of people clamoring to stay here, and we'll have a ton of customers. More than we could ever hope to host."

Harold let out a sniff. "You're going to ruin the forest. Stone won't have a place to live."

Ellison cleared his throat as he approached his gardener and the typhon. "So PJ and Grant were right. You are friends with this…erm…person." He swallowed, clearly unnerved by the creature but trying not to appear that way. "I wish you'd told me."

Harold scoffed, but Stone gently nudged him with his pinky nail (which was the size of Harold's head). "My old man said it was important to keep Stone safe. And with the queen, then you bringing all these strangers, we gotta make sure—"

"If it would help," Andres said lightly, "His Majesty would be happy to release a royal decree making this forest as an official sanctuary for Mister…Stone, is it?" He tilted his head up at the typhon. "I know in years past, they made sport of hunting your kind, but I can assure you that the king and his soldiers will have no patience for that sort of thing."

Harold visibly relaxed, and, PJ couldn't believe it, a smile appeared. He now bore a striking resemblance to Stone, though PJ couldn't even fathom how they could possibly be related.

"Well, if that's all," Andres said. "I've got two

spies and an incredibly powerful amulet to take back to King's Capital in the morning. Are there any more revelations that need to come to light?" He looked around at the rest expectantly, and thankfully, no one spoke up. "Excellent. I'll be back at the camp, if anyone—"

"Wait!" Ingrid said. "Why don't you come to our potluck tonight?"

"Ingrid, we don't even have a tavern anymore," Bill said.

"We can make do." Ingrid smiled at everyone. "I think it's time we officially open the Forest Den Holiday Town."

"What about us?" Adonna asked. "Are we still unwelcome here, Ellison?"

"Of course you're welcome," Pat said, his tail wagging. "That's what makes it a potluck. Everyone brings something. I'm sure you've got a great skill you could bring to the table."

"I'm a baker," Adonna said. "I've got a few loaves—they might not be the freshest, but—"

"Oh, we lost our baker!" Audra said with a smile to her wife. "How fortunate you're just outside the forest."

"And I'm a butcher," Ulysses said, stepping forward. "I've got some beef I could donate to the cause."

Chatter broke out at once, with everyone talking

amongst themselves as they came up with a plan. PJ couldn't help but notice Kishan inching away, looking for all the world like a man who'd lost everything.

"Where are you going?" PJ asked, walking over to him.

"I mean, it's clear I'm no longer welcome," Kishan said. "Ellison's furious with me. And the rest of them…" He gestured toward the crowd. "I suppose I'd always planned on leaving, but… Guess I'll have to figure out some other way to make my money."

"You know," Grant said, inching over. "There are gonna be a lot of magical folks coming through this town."

"Yeah, and?"

"And they might need some entertainment," Grant continued, wagging his eyebrows. "I'm sure you could get your magic tricks from the forest, set up some kind of act. Probably make a pretty decent living."

Kishan opened and closed his mouth. "Do you think they'd allow me to do that after what I did?"

PJ shrugged. "Only one way to find out."

Chapter Twenty-Two

As dusk descended on the forest, the hodgepodge group worked together to get the potluck meal started. The Cheshireville group had returned to their businesses to retrieve supplies for the potluck, and the soldiers, who'd brought Oscar and Roe along in an iron-barred carriage, stood around talking amongst themselves. Several mentioned that they'd had family or friends who'd been in one of these enclaves, while others had just heard about them but never seen them.

The townsfolk—both Forest Den and Cheshireville—worked together to assemble a meal in no time. With Adonna's bread and Pat's potatoes and meat from Ulysses's butcher shop grilled on a spit that Bill constructed, complemented by salads that Orlena helped Ingrid put together, and several casks of Brennan's cider that Stone was able to help move *very* quickly, before long, everyone was ready to eat.

"Hm," Andres said, looking at the crushed mushrooms as Ellison described how they'd been an outdoor tavern. He had the amulet box under his arm (he'd wisely decided not to let anyone else handle it). "Henderson?"

One of the soldiers perked up and strolled over, saluting his leader with a stiff movement. "Yes, sir?"

"You're a green witch, aren't you?"

"Yes sir. What do you need me to do?"

"Can you regrow these mushrooms?" Andres asked.

The soldier stepped forward and put his hands to the ground. Green tendrils of magic shot out from his fingertips, sliding through the dirt and reaching out toward the mushrooms. The caps fell in on themselves, disintegrating into nothing, but in their place, new mushrooms emerged, growing and expanding as if time itself had sped up. Triple the number of mushroom chairs and tables emerged, creating enough space for everyone who'd be coming to dinner.

"Does this work?" the green witch asked.

Ellison squealed and clapped. "Oh, it's amazing. It's perfect!"

The green witch blushed and saluted Andres before returning to his post to watch Roe and Oscar.

"Guess that means we won't have to eat at Kishan's," Grant said, walking up beside PJ. "Though I'm a bit disappointed it was the innkeeper. I thought they were supposed to be upstanding individuals who help the town and do no wrong."

"Even Bev has her secrets," PJ said with a shrug.

"You know what?" Ellison said, counting the heads. "We don't have enough utensils. Unless someone can magic them out of thin air."

"Kishan probably does," Adonna said. "If someone wants to find him."

"I'm here." Kishan arrived with a hand-drawn wagon laden with supplies, including plates, bowls, tankards, and cutlery. PJ was actually surprised to see him come back, as he'd assumed Kishan would've packed up and left. But the promise of sticking around and fixing what he'd broken clearly appealed to him, even though the Forest Den crowd gave him an evil eye. But Ellison, with a little goading from PJ, approached the innkeeper after a long, pregnant pause.

"Thank you for bringing all this," he said stiffly.

"Consider it my donation to the holiday town,"

Kishan said, his gaze on the ground. "As well as the start of my formal apology for all the trouble I caused."

No one spoke for a few minutes, then, surprisingly, Harold spoke up from his perch by Bill's door.

"Well, as long as you're really sorry," he said sincerely. "Suppose nothing bad really happened."

"Except we lost half the town," Ingrid said, still glaring at Kishan. "And a tree fell over. And you cut a branch off an old tree that didn't deserve it. All because you wanted to make some coin and didn't want to ask for help. Because you thought the lot of us would steal from you or do something with the amulet."

"In his defense," Andres said, "it's quite the amulet. And he's not wrong that it would be tempting for anyone who longed for more power."

"Hear, hear," PJ said with a firm nod. To Andres's confused look, he added, "I can feel it from all the way over here. Keep that in the box, will you?"

"We're all having to break bread with people we once considered enemies," Andres said. "I think it's best for everyone if we start now. Especially considering that if Kishan hadn't come, we'd otherwise be eating and drinking straight off the platter."

The crowd moved slowly, but before long, things were humming once again as dinner came together. With plates and tankards and new mushrooms and a full spread for dinner, the soldiers and townsfolk gathered to share the fruits of their labor. There were easy smiles, delicious food, and Kishan even had enough courage (or cider) to get up and perform a few magic tricks for the crowd. PJ had to admit—he was good at his craft. Even though he knew the secrets, he was still astonished when Kishan was able to throw his voice to the other side of the forest.

"I can see how he was able to make us think there was a typhon roaming about," Ingrid said. "But a magician like this would surely be an excellent addition to our advertising, right, Ellison?"

"I suppose." Ellison still seemed put out by Kishan but looked to be softening, especially as his holiday town plans looked to be unencumbered.

PJ could see the vision. To be able to come here, to experience the warmth of these people and the camaraderie after the long years of discord with the queen—that could absolutely be worth a few gold coins, especially as the forest came to life around them, with magical orbs dancing in the dark skies above.

"So I guess we're hitting the road tomorrow, hm?" Grant asked, jarring PJ from his thoughts.

"What?"

"I mean," Grant shrugged, "unless you want to have another holiday. Test out the place for Ellison. Give some feedback. I can't say I *want* to leave, but we probably should, eh?"

PJ frowned. This was the third time he'd been startled to realize their job was done and it was time to say goodbye—and it wasn't getting any easier.

"I guess so," PJ said, unable to keep the sadness from his voice. "We could stay, but…"

"You don't seem too happy about moving on," Andres said, coming to sit next to them. "You've done a wonderful thing here, you know. This town and these people are better for your presence."

"We're glad to do it," PJ said. "But you know, it can get a little lonely, having to make friends just to leave them."

"Ah." Andres nodded knowingly. "That can be tough. But I did a bit of traveling around the country myself during the queen's reign. And I found that as big as this continent is, it can be quite small in other ways. I can't tell you how often I'd be in a remote town like this and run into someone I know."

PJ nodded, a little lightness edging into his somber mood. "That's true. We knew some of the witches who lived here before Kishan scared everyone."

"And the ogres," Grant added. "They're the

reason we came here in the first place, remember?"

"See?" Andres squeezed PJ's shoulder. "The more you travel, the more you realize that the entire country is your community. People are pretty similar everywhere you go. They just want a chance to live, to enjoy their property, and to have community with others." He gestured around them to the chattering group that had come together in a matter of hours. "The work you're doing, if it's anything like this, is going to do great things for Kingscountry. The world needs young men like you doing the work bringing people together. Even if it does mean you'll have to leave before seeing the fruits of your labor."

"Besides that," Grant said, "you're not leaving *all* your friends. I'm still here. Tim's here. And you know you can't get rid of us, even if you wanted to." He glanced at Andres. "But do me a favor and *don't* mention you saw me to Dane. I don't want him," he blanched, "being *proud* of me or anything."

Andres laughed. "I'll be sure to keep your involvement under wraps. But if you boys would do me a favor and stop by our encampment before heading out, I might have something you want to see."

When there was nothing else to talk about, the party dispersed, with Ingrid and Ellison walking the

Cheshireville folks back out to the village, and the rest of the Forest Den contingent cleaning up and calling it a night. PJ and Grant had opted to stay in the forest one more night—just to make sure nothing else was amiss. But as PJ fell asleep, he could sense that amulet pulsing in the distance from where it rested under Andres's head.

In the morning, PJ still wasn't ready to leave. Although his conversation with Andres had bolstered his confidence, it was sad to bid everyone farewell. The Forest Den folks gathered to send them off, making sure they'd eaten breakfast and had a spot of Ingrid's tea for energy. There were tears, hugs, and more thanks, as well as promises that PJ and Grant would make their way back to the haven to spend a few days (and coins).

Then the boys had to pass through Cheshireville, where they were met by Ellison, who had a basket of goods from the rest of town, including no fewer than six custards from Adonna. He also told them to come back when they were in the area, and to share the good parts of their stay with folks they saw on the road.

"We'll be sure to mention it to everyone we see," Grant said.

With their goodbyes said, there was one more stop to make at the encampment just beyond the town. The soldiers had finished packing up, with their horses laden with all their supplies. Roe and Oscar remained in the barred wagon, scowling at the boys as they walked past. PJ could vaguely sense the amulet somewhere at the front of the queue and wisely kept his distance.

Andres waved them over. "Ah, I'm glad you boys made it. We've got to get on our way back to King's Capital, and I didn't want to leave without saying goodbye." He held out his hand to shake theirs. "I wanted to formally thank you, on behalf of the king, for the work you're doing. And to offer you a small token of his esteem." He reached into his pocket and handed them a purse of gold coins. "I know it can't be easy, traveling as you are without any way to make any money. But hopefully—"

"We don't need it," PJ said, sliding it back into Andres's hands, earning a pout from Grant. "My, erm, own amulet has been providing me all the gold we need."

"Ah." Andres smiled. "I heard about the dragon's hoard, but I've never seen it."

"That makes two of us," PJ said. "Coins kinda just appear in my pocket when I need them."

"Handy." Andres pocketed the purse. "But I do hope you'll take this letter I received this morning. I wasn't sure I'd get it in time, but I'm happy to say I did." He flashed PJ a smile as he handed the sealed envelope over. "Don't ask me questions about it, because I absolutely won't answer them."

The letter had their names in pretty script that looked familiar. "Thank you," PJ said with a smile. "Safe journey back to King's Capital."

"As I said, this country isn't so big that we won't cross paths again," Andres said, climbing up onto his horse. "I look forward to hearing more about your exploits in the coming months." He put his fingers to his mouth and whistled, alerting the cadre of soldiers, and they moved as a unit away from the town, Roe and Oscar teetering along with them.

"Don't ask questions," Grant muttered, looking over PJ's shoulder at the letter. "Well? Let's see. Maybe it's a summons to solve a problem in King's Capital. Wouldn't that be something, eh?"

PJ shrugged and opened the wax-sealed envelope, unfolding it.

As soon as his gaze fell on the signature, he gasped, a smile coming to his face.

Dear PJ,

I was so happy to get a letter from Andres telling me he'd run into you. Word had passed through the Pigsend grapevine that you'd left school under not-great circumstances, but I had faith you wouldn't have done so lightly.

We've all been so thrilled to get your letters about your new adventures. Magic has certainly opened doors in this world that make things easier, even as so many things have gotten harder, too.

I always knew you were destined for greater things, and not just because of that dragon lurking in your mind. You've got a good heart, a smart brain, and a desire to make things right. I'm so happy that Grant's with you, too. For all his quirks, he's got a quick mind and seizes any opportunity he can. That's important when turning strangers into friends—and trying to uncover secrets they'd rather leave buried. The two of you make a great team, I'm sure, and the world is a better place with you helping it along.

I do hope you'll eventually make your way back to Pigsend, though I know there are plenty of problems that could be solved by a brilliant dragon shifter and his best friend in the tumultuous world we live in. In the meantime, please consider letting your parents (and Vicky, of course) know how to return correspondence to you. If memory serves, I believe there was an address the grannies gave you.

We're all eagerly awaiting your next letter to hear what wonderful things you've done in Cheshireville. Take care of yourselves and each other, and we'll see you when we see you.

All my love,
Bev

PS: Biscuit says hi, too!

PJ looked up at the sound of someone sniffing. He frowned when he realized Grant's eyes were misty as he rubbed his nose.

"Darn it, Bev," he said, his voice thick.

"I didn't even think of my parents writing to the grannies to get letters to me," PJ said, shaking his head. "I wonder how that works? I mean, the letters go to the grannies, of course, but how do they get to me?"

"They'd probably come out through the amulet, wouldn't you think?" Grant said, peering at the soldiers disappearing in the distance. "So do we want to know how Bev was able to get a letter to Andres so fast or…?"

"You heard the man." PJ chuckled. "We can ask questions, but we won't get any answers. Suppose if we do want the truth, we'll have to head to Pigsend to get it."

"Ah, eventually," Grant said. "I don't like that our 'adventures' have been through the grapevine. I'm sure Etheldra's been griping about how she always knew we were ne'er-do-wells."

PJ inspected the letter again. There was something soothing about knowing she was proud of him—much like knowing his own parents were brimming with joy about him helping the world. It made him incredibly homesick, but at the same time…his cause had never felt more right.

"Well, shall we head back toward Pigsend? Check out the ol' homestead and see what kind of problems we can find there?" Grant asked.

PJ carefully folded the letter and tucked it away. "No. Not yet. We've been to three towns so far, and haven't even come close to a dragon shifter. I doubt we missed one back home."

"Yeah, and I'm sure there's another small, helpless town with magical problems who needs our help," Grant said. "Shall we?"

"Let's hit the road."

ACKNOWLEGMENTS

As always, first thanks goes to my husband, for supporting me, believing in me, and being my rock during the difficult season of two very small children and me trying to take on the world. Thanks must also go to my parents, my in-laws, and my aunt for being the world's best village and allowing me to keep writing with said very small children.

Thanks to Chelsea, Danielle, Lisa, and Lacey for being the all-star team who helps bring these beautiful books to life.

Thanks go to the Sush Street Team for being the cheerleaders who love these books and continue to read everything I put out.

And finally, and most ardently, thanks to you, the reader, for buying, loving, and sharing my cozy little stories about Bev, Lillie, and now PJ. I'm so grateful I stumbled into this wonderful niche, and that it's brought you as much joy as it's brought me.

ALSO BY THE AUTHOR

THE POBYD PERFECTIONS BAKERY SERIES

Lillie Dean, a magical baker from Pigsend, is off on her own adventures in the seaside town of Silverkeep. But her somewhat villainous past has come back to haunt her, and now she must figure out who's sending threatening letters to the magical creatures in town before the town descends into chaos.

Available in eBook, Audiobook, Paperback, and Hardcover

A MER-MURDER AT THE COVE, A PARANORMAL COZY MYSTERY SERIES

Jo Maelstrom's avoidance problems hit an all-time high when, after weeks of dodging her grandmother's calls, she got a text that "Big Jo" had died suddenly. Now back in Eldred's Hollow, a supernatural haven on the Gulf Coast of Alabama, Jo is forced to reckon with her past – and the severe lack of magic that sent her running in the first place. Her grandmother's bar and marina, Witch's Cove, is in some dire financial straits, and there's more than a few people itching to take it off her hands. But when the leader of the local mermaid clan washes up dead on the shore, Jo finds herself embroiled in the question of who and why – and does it have anything to do with her own grandmother's mysterious death?

A Mer-Murder at the Cove is the first book in the Witch's Cove Paranormal Cozy Mystery series. Available in eBook and Paperback

Also By The Author

EMPATH

Lauren Dailey is in break-up hell, but if you ask her she's doing just great. She hears a mysterious voice promising an easy escape from her problems and finds herself in a brand new world where she has the power to feel what others are feeling. Just one problem—there's a dragon in the mountains that happens to eat Empaths. And it might be the source of the mysterious voice tempting her deeper into her own darkness.

Empath is a stand-alone fantasy available now in eBook, Paperback, and Hardcover.

About the Author

S. Usher Evans was born and raised in Pensacola, Florida. After a decade of fighting bureaucratic battles as an IT consultant in Washington, DC, she suffered a massive quarter-life-crisis. She found fighting dragons was more fun than writing policy, so she moved back to Pensacola to write books full-time. She currently resides there with her husband and kids, and frequently can be found plotting on the beach.

Visit S. Usher Evans online at:
http://www.susherevans.com/

www.ingramcontent.com/pod-product-compliance
Lightning Source LLC
Chambersburg PA
CBHW021036310726
48969CB00006B/1672